The Mystery of the
ALAMO
GHOST

by
Carole Marsh

Published by Gallopade International/Carole Marsh Books. Printed in the United States of America.

Cover design: Vicki DeJoy; Editor: Jenny Corsey; Graphic Design: Steve St. Laurent; Layout and footer design: Lynette Rowe; Photography: Amanda McCutcheon.

Also available:
The Mystery of the Alamo Ghost Teacher's Guide
1,000 Readers – Davy Crockett: Legendary Frontiersman
1,000 Readers – Sam Houston: Courageous Father of Texas

Gallopade International is introducing SAT words that kids need to know in each new book that we publish. The SAT words are bold in the story. Look for this special logo beside each word in the glossary. Happy Learning!

Gallopade is proud to be a member and supporter of these educational organizations and associations:

American Booksellers Association
American Library Association
International Reading Association
National Association for Gifted Children
The National School Supply and Equipment Association
The National Council for the Social Studies
Museum Store Association
Association of Partners for Public Lands
Association of Booksellers for Children
Association for the Study of African American Life and History
National Alliance of Black School Educators

This book is dedicated to the people of San Antonio, who have such a lovely city that they share so well.

This book is a complete work of fiction. All events are fictionalized, and although the first names of real children are used, their characterization in this book is fiction.

For additional information on
Carole Marsh Mysteries, visit:
www.carolemarshmysteries.com

Grant in his coonskin cap

30 YEARS AGO . . .

As a mother and an author, one of the fondest periods of my life was when I decided to write mystery books for children. At this time (1979) kids were pretty much glued to the TV, something parents and teachers complained about the way they do about video games today.

I decided to set each mystery in a real place—a place kids could go and visit for themselves after reading the book. And I also used real children as characters. Usually a couple of my own children served as characters, and I had no trouble recruiting kids from the book's location to also be characters.

Also, I wanted all the kids—boys and girls of all ages—to participate in solving the mystery. And, I wanted kids to learn something as they read. Something about the history of the location. And I wanted the stories to be funny.

That formula of real+scary+smart+fun served me well. The kids and I had a great time visiting each site, and many of the events in the stories actually came out of our experiences there.

I love getting letters from teachers and parents who say they read the book with their class or child, then visited the historic site and saw all the places in the mystery for themselves. What's so great about that? What's great is that you and your children have an experience that bonds you together forever. Something you shared. Something you both cared about at the time. Something that crossed all age levels—a good story, a good scare, a good laugh!

30 years later,

Carole Marsh

Christina Yother   **Grant Yother**   **Ashley Nuqui**   **Seve Nuqui**

ABOUT THE CHARACTERS

Christina Yother, 10, from Peachtree City, Georgia

Grant Yother, 7, from Peachtree City, Georgia
Christina's brother

Ashley Nuqui as Rose, 12, from Peachtree City, Georgia

Seve Nuqui as Juan, 10, Rose's brother, from
Peachtree City, Georgia

The many places featured in the book actually exist and
are worth a visit! Perhaps you could read the book and follow
the trail these kids went on during their mysterious
adventure!

Titles in the Carole Marsh Mysteries Series

Books and Teacher's Guides are available at booksellers, libraries, school supply stores, museums, and many other locations!

CONTENTS

1 ALAMO HERE WE GO!

"Remember the Alamo!" Grant shouted—right in the middle of Atlanta Hartsfield-Jackson International Airport in Atlanta, Georgia. Grant Yother was only seven, and so, his sister Christina guessed, he was too young to know not to scream in the airport.

"Grant!" she cried, grabbing him by the sleeve of his dinosaur vest which was made like a safari jacket with netting and even had a plastic toy stegosaurus and T-Rex strapped to it. "If you scream like that you might get us arrested. It's the time of terrorism, you know."

Her brother pulled away. He squatted down and raised his arms and hands into claws and said, "Arrrrrgggggggg!" in his best imitation of a dinosaur. Sometimes, Christina thought, she believed her brother thought he really was a dinosaur. "And just what time is that oh sister of mine?"

Atlanta Hartsfield-Jackson
Airport

Houston Hobby
Airport

In spite of herself, Christina giggled. She adored her brother, but he was so silly. "Don't you read the papers or watch the news? Airport security is tight these days. You're supposed to behave yourself."

Mimi and Papa came running up behind their two grandchildren. They had been stopped in the security check line because Papa's big, shiny, black cowboy boots set off the alarm–just like they always did (they had metal in the heels)–even when he insisted they would not. He always had to take off his big longhorn belt buckle too. In fact, thought Christina, Papa almost had to undress to get through the security line every time. It was sooooo embarrassing!

"Not likely," said Papa, scrubbing his knuckles over Grant's runaway blond curls.

"Not likely what?" asked Mimi, out of breath from running to catch up with the kids. She had her computer in one hand, and a raincoat, umbrella, and purse in the other. Papa carried all their tickets.

"Not likely that Grant's going to behave," Papa teased. "That's not really the job of a rambunctious seven-year-old, you know."

"Not if he takes after you!" said Mimi. Papa had a reputation for acting pretty wild and crazy for a grown up.

Atlanta Hartsfield-Jackson
Airport

Houston Hobby
Airport

"And what about a nine-year-old girl?" Christina asked primly. She had the reputation of a know-it-all, which was ok, she figured, because she really did know a lot. She couldn't help that, could she?

Mimi gave her granddaughter a playful grin and a wink. "Now you know it's the job of the women in this family to walk the straight and narrow and be little ladies all the time."

That made Papa roar with laughter. Mimi was pretty wild and crazy herself, which made Grant and Christina love to go off on jaunts with their grandparents–especially if it involved missing a day of school, which (unfortunately!) being spring break, this trip did not.

Mimi wrote kid's books, mysteries mostly, and often used her grandkids (and neighbors' kids, and kids who read her books, and most anyone else between ages 7 and 14 she could get her hands on) as "real" characters in her books. Then she set the story of the book in a real location. This time, it was the Alamo. They were on their way to San Antonio, Texas. And, if they didn't hurry up, they were going to miss their plane.

"Get along little doggies!" Papa shouted, urging them all to move faster toward the train that would take

Atlanta Hartsfield-Jackson
Airport

Houston Hobby
Airport

them to Gate 13. Papa always sounded like a cowboy. His business card even had Trail Boss on it as his title.

"Arf! Arf! ARF!! ARF!!!" Grant barked, now poised like a galloping puppy. Great, thought Christina—some people have a brother; I have a dino dog.

"Whoopie-kai-yai-yea!" hollered Papa as the train doors swooshed open and gobbled them inside. Everyone grabbed a pole to hold onto to keep their footing as the train roared off.

"Uh, Mimi . . ." Christina said, giving her grandmother "the look."

"What?" asked Mimi, then looked down and realized her colorful Cirque-du-Soleil umbrella was poking Christina in the stomach. "Oh, sorry."

"I don't need a new bellybutton," Christina said.

"Oh, why not?" said Mimi, gently poking the rounded point of the umbrella in strategic spots where she knew her granddaughter was especially ticklish. Christina tried to grab and cover all those spots at once, while laughing so hard a tear formed in the corner of her eye.

"Why do you have all that rain gear, anyway, Mimi?" she asked. "Papa says it's going to be 101 degrees in San Antonio. I don't think it's gonna rain there."

Atlanta Hartsfield-Jackson
Airport

Houston Hobby
Airport

"You never know," Mimi said. Of course, that's what Mimi always said. Christina guessed that was her mystery state of mind. She recognized that absentminded look her grandmother always got as she headed toward her next mystery book site. Christina knew that she was always writing in her head. The weird thing was that some of the things her grandmother/writer made up often came true. That, to Christina, was pretty strange and scary. What, she wondered, would happen on this mystery trip adventure? Last time, when Mimi was writing a mystery book during the Boston Marathon, their runner/schoolteacher/cousin Priscilla was kidnapped off the racecourse—right in front of their eyes!

Suddenly, the train stopped and spit them out right at the escalator. "Run!" cried Papa, checking his watch. They all dashed up the escalator and ran toward Gate 13. Everyone was boarding, and they were even calling standbys to give them any leftover seats.

"I hope they don't give our seats away," Christina worried aloud.

"Aw, don't worry," Grant said. "You can have my seat. I'll ride up front in the cockpit. In fact, the pilot can have my seat. I'll sit in his and fly us to

Atlanta Hartsfield-Jackson
Airport

Houston Hobby
Airport

San Antonio." Grant now took on the pose of an airplane and zoomed around the waiting area as Papa checked them in.

"And we'd end up in Timbuktu," said Christina.

"Yeah, Tim Buck can go too," Grant said.

"Grant, you're incorrigible!" his sister said.

That stopped her brother cold. He froze in his airplane pose, arms outstretched. "Incorrigible? Incorrigible? Hey, that sounds like a compliment to me," he said.

Christina gave him her famous "look" that meant get-off-my-case-leave-me-alone-don't-be-so-stupid-I-don't-know-you-I-am-not-with-these-people-never-seen-them-before. Then she stared at the ceiling.

"Uh, Christina?" Papa said gently. "Going with us?"

Christina looked up and blushed. She realized she had been standing there daydreaming while everyone had boarded but her and Papa. "Uh, sure," she said, ducking past the gate agent and lugging her purple backpack down the corridor to the airplane. As she crossed the threshold over that creepy place where the airplane doesn't quite meet the ramp—where you can see the ground below and air swishes all around you—Christina noted the number of the airplane: 1313. She quickly jumped inside the aircraft and handed the

Atlanta Hartsfield-Jackson
Airport

Houston Hobby
Airport

flight attendant her seat pass. The woman smiled at her. "Your row is number 13," she said merrily, pointing the way.

Christina felt the tiny hairs on her arms and neck stand up like little soldiers. Goosebumps formed beneath them. Of course, her row *would* be "lucky" number 13, she thought.

Mimi, Papa, and Grant were already strapping themselves into their seats.

"Peanuts! Peanuts!! Bring on the peanuts!!! Gotta have peanuts!!!!" Grant said to any and all who would listen. He was now in a monkey pose, scratching his ribs and underarms like an ape. The people around them giggled.

"Do I have to sit beside him?" Christina asked her grandmother. "Couldn't we have checked him as baggage?"

Before Mimi could answer, a flight attendant appeared behind Christina and took her backpack. "Please sit down, young lady, we're about to take off." She sounded stern. Christina was sooooo embarrassed. She plopped into her seat and buckled up. The lady handed her the backpack with a smile that was not really a smile.

Christina snuggled back into the seat and tried to disappear.

Atlanta Hartsfield-Jackson Airport

Houston Hobby Airport

"I think I could eat a peanut, folks," Grant said to no one in particular.

"I think there could be a ghost in this mystery," Mimi said into thin air. She was looking at the blank movie screen as though only she could see a film playing.

"I think I'll take a nap," said Papa, who was sitting on the other side of Christina. He leaned back and tilted his big, black cowboy hat down over his face.

"Hey, Papa," Christina said. "You made our reservations at the hotel?"

"Naturally," said Papa from under his hat.

"Well, do you know our room number?" Mimi always had to have a special room to write in. She said she couldn't write in just any old room; she needed a desk with a window and some sunshine and a decent view, and no orange bedspread—never ever.

Papa half snorted a snore. "Sure . . ." he droned, and then got silent. Just when Christina thought he had gone to sleep and would not answer her question, Papa's hat quivered. "Thirteen . . . we're staying in Room 13."

"Well of course we are," Christina muttered under her breath. This, she felt, was going to be the mystery-trip-from–you-know-where.

"Here," said Grant. He was handing Christina a peanut when the airplane hit some turbulence and

Atlanta Hartsfield-Jackson
Airport

Houston Hobby
Airport

caused his arm to bounce. That's when he stuck the peanut up his sister's nose.

"Argggggggg!" Christina cried.

"Is that a dino arggggggg or a dog arggggggg, sister?" Grant asked.

Atlanta Hartsfield-Jackson Airport

Houston Hobby Airport

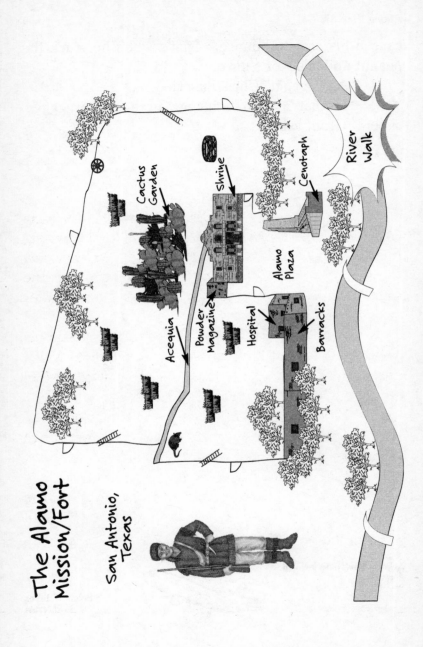

2 ALAMO ALÁ MODE

When the plane landed in Houston, Christina could see that Mimi was right, as usual. It was pouring rain! The tarmac glistened like wet licorice, and Christina hated licorice; she never could stand the anise flavoring, even though she loved most other spices—especially hot ones.

While Papa went to get the baggage (he said he could do it easier without all the "extra baggage" which Christina figured meant them) and rent a car, Mimi herded them to a kiosk that sold ice cream.

"I'll have pistachio please," said Christina.

"I'll have butter pecan with a little hot fudge sauce and some whipped cream," Mimi said.

"I'll have Alamo Alá Mode," said Grant.

Christina punched her little brother in the shoulder. "Grant, there's no such thing," she told him.

Houston Hobby
Airport

Texas
Countryside

"Is too!" he countered, pointing to the menu overhead. Sure enough, in big, bold letters with a fat peanut wearing a cowboy hat beside it was Alamo Alá Mode.

Christina groaned, and they all crowded around one of those tiny ice cream parlor tables with the chairs with the heart-shaped backs. Mimi plopped all her rain gear on the extra chair, and they all began to lick away.

"Christina," Mimi finally said between slurps, "You don't seem very excited about this trip. I thought you would love Texas. I'm counting on you, you know, for your valuable history mystery input."

Christina continued to swirl her tongue around the mound of mint green ice cream. When her taste buds felt like they had frozen solid, she answered her grandmother. "Well, I guess this just seems like boy history. You know, missions, and forts, and fighting, and Davy Crockett, and all that jazz. I'd rather forget the Alamo and go shopping or something."

Mimi seemed disappointed. Her granddaughter was usually gung ho for almost anything—especially a mystery. Maybe all she needed was a little persuasion.

"Don't you know the story of the Alamo is one of the most exciting in American history?"

Houston Hobby
Airport

Texas
Countryside

Mimi reminded Christina. "It's a wild and crazy story of murder, mayhem, heroes, freedom, revenge, and silver."

"Well, when you put it that way . . . " Christina began thoughtfully.

Grant interrupted. "Well, I plan to remember Alamo Alá Mode ice cream for the rest of my life. It's super!"

"C'mon, peanut breath," Mimi teased him. "I see Papa waving his cowboy hat over there by the baggage carousel. I think he wants us to move along, little doggies."

"Carousel?" Grant turned and looked around for a merry-go-round to ride.

"Not that kind of carousel," Christina said, reading her brother's mind. "Mimi means the conveyor belt that your luggage comes out on from the airplane."

Grant looked disappointed, but instead of arguing he flew towards Papa and the mountain of luggage.

Christina followed her grandmother, calling, "What about the rest of the Alamo story?" But Mimi was already out of earshot.

Before she could ask any more questions, the luggage was loaded into a bright red SUV and Papa,

Houston Hobby
Airport

Texas
Countryside

complaining because no one had bothered to buy him any ice cream, was speeding down the highway toward San Antonio—home of the Alamo.

Houston Hobby
Airport

Texas
Countryside

3 BLUEBONNETS AND LONGHORNS

In spite of herself, Christina was fascinated by the Texas countryside. It was early spring, and the bluebonnets were in bloom. Christina thought the carpets of lavender spread out as far as she could see on each side of the car were beautiful. That was always one of the best things about travel, she thought. You got to see sights that you had never seen before. And you could never guess what they would be. Like Mimi's mysteries, they would pop out and surprise you just when you would least expect it.

Suddenly, Grant starting screaming for Papa to stop the car. "Look!" he hollered as Papa pulled off onto the gravel shoulder of the road.

"What?" said Papa.

"What, Grant?" asked Mimi.

"Gotta go?" asked Christina.

Texas Countryside

Let's Eat BBQ!

"No," said Grant, irritably. "Look at those cows. They have white bones sticking out of the side of their heads."

Papa laughed. "Those are longhorn cattle," he explained. "Those are their horns."

"Yeah, Grant, Texas cows," Christina said, and Mimi and Papa both laughed. Christina's least favorite thing was when adults laughed, and she didn't know why.

Papa pulled back on the road and before they could settle down, he skidded right back off into the parking lot of a dumpy, weatherbeaten cabin that Mimi called a barbecue joint.

"Is this place on fire, or what?" asked Grant, as they climbed out of the car.

"That's the barbecue pit," said Papa. "I'll bet they've been smoking this stuff all night." He rubbed his stomach.

Everyone ordered barbecue sandwiches with thick slabs of beef covered in glistening red sauce and bright green pickles. Each order came with steaming baked beans, french fries, and glasses of iced tea the size of pitchers.

As they sat outdoors at a rickety picnic table, Christina tried again. "Tell us the story of the Alamo, Mimi."

Texas
Countryside

Let's Eat
BBQ!

Mimi wiped a streak of red sauce from her upper lip. She shook her bright blond hair and put on her history teacher look. Christina hoped she wouldn't give more of an answer than she had bargained for, but as usual, Mimi surprised her. "Yes," she began, as though she were in the middle of a story. "Davy Crockett, the famous (killed a bear/didn't kill a bear/who knows) American frontiersman was there. So was Jim Bowie, the guy (or was it his brother?) who invented the famous Bowie knife. And Santa Anna, the great dictator of Mexico, and one walloping battle."

"And the good guys won?" said Christina, already bored.

Mimi, Papa, and Grant all gave Christina a surprised and mysterious look. "No," said Mimi quietly. "They lost."

Now Christina really was confused. She sat in the back seat all the rest of the way past the blue haze of bluebonnets pondering why a battle someone lost got so famous. Failure. Defeat. She just didn't get it. What was the rest of the story, she wondered, and when would Mimi finally share it with her?

Let's Eat BBQ!

San Antonio

Grant squealed every time he saw a longhorn, so he squealed a lot all the way to San Antonio. It was late afternoon when they arrived in the city. Papa drove right up to the front of the hotel, saying he was tired and was going to use the valet parking.

"Valley parking?" said Grant. "There's no valley around here—the place is flat as an armadillo pancake." That's what Grant had taken to calling the grayish green funny-looking creatures squashed by the side of the road.

"Vah-LAY," Christina said, phonetically. "It's French for when a nice guy opens your door and parks the car and brings it again when you want it." Once more Mimi and Papa laughed and Christina wondered why. Was she a stand-up comic, or something?

But she didn't have time to ponder the situation, because as they paraded through the hotel doors, a man in a prison suit said, "Good evening—you're under arrest!"

Let's Eat BBQ!

San Antonio

4 JUST SEND OUR MAIL … TO THE SAN ANTONIO JAIL

Christina and Grant looked at one another in shock, but it all turned out to be one big pun. The hotel was the former San Antonio jail. Now it looked like a hotel, except you were "booked" into your "cell" by "officers" at a front desk that had bars like an old-timey police station. The bellman, also in a black and white striped prisoner's suit, escorted them to their cell/room.

Christina was relieved to see that it was really just an ordinary hotel room. TV, cable, fridge, microwave, hairdryer, and all the other essentials.

As the bellman put their bags away, he said, "We'll keep you under lock and key, but if you want out on parole, just call me. On the last day of your stay, you'll find a note with the amount of your bail under

San Antonio
"Jail"

Cell
13

your door." As he left, he added, "I hope you find your sentence very enjoyable."

When the door closed behind him, they all fell on the beds laughing. "That's so silly!" said Papa.

"I thought it was sort of cool," said Mimi, who loved puns anyway.

Suddenly, Grant's smile turned to a frown. "Are we really under arrest?" he asked.

"I'm going to get some ice," said Christina. When she left the room, the door slammed behind her. She turned, planning to knock and ask for a key to let herself back in when she spotted the black numbers on the door—13.

"Oh, yeah," Christina muttered to herself as she sashayed down the hall with the ice bucket. "An unlucky number, boy history, and rain rain rain—what kind of trip is this going to be?"

Suddenly an arm reached out and grabbed her by the wrist and pulled her inside the small room with the ice machine. "A very scary one, kid!" a voice hissed in her ear.

San Antonio
"Jail"

Cell
13

I've been grabbed!

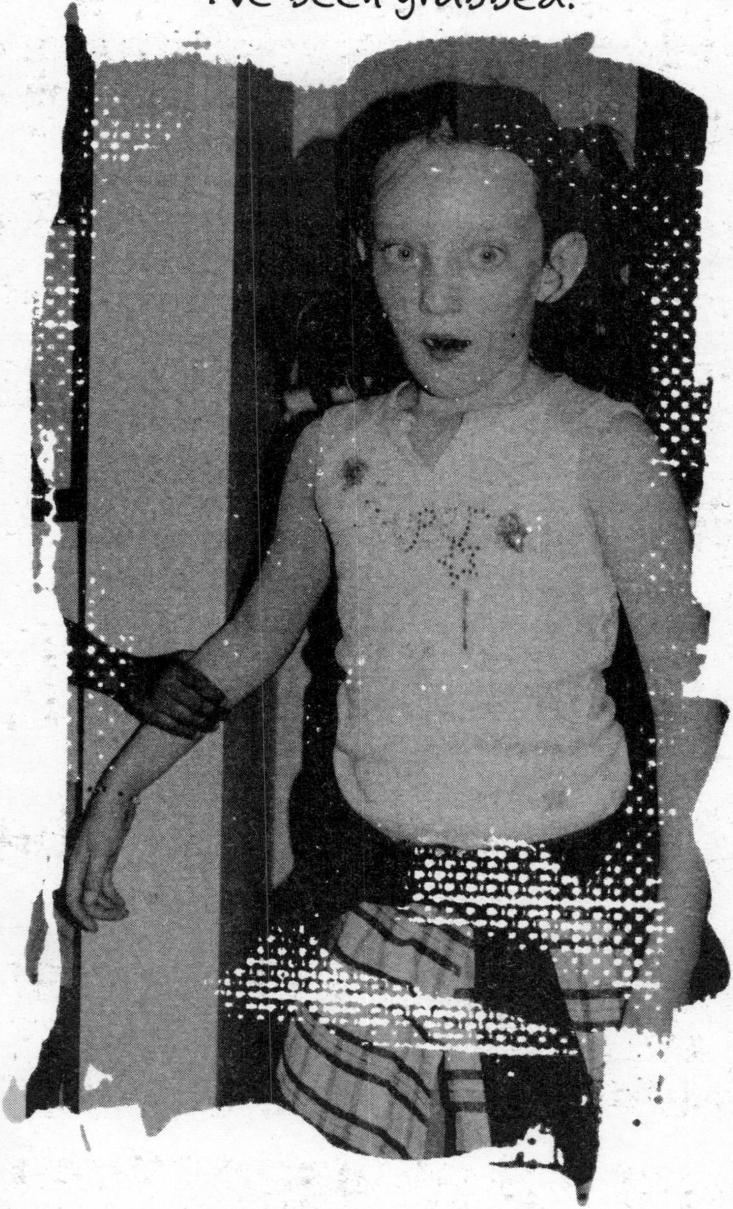

5 HISTORY'S A MYSTERY TO ME

"Who are you?!" Christina demanded with a yelp. The boy, who had grabbed her, and a girl who had come in behind him, both doubled over in laughter.

"Don't you know?" asked the girl, as the boy tugged the ice bucket from Christina's hand and filled it for her.

Christina shook her head no. She was totally confused and mightily irritated.

"I'm Juan," said the boy, grabbing Christina's hand and shaking it. His hand was cold and wet. Very gross.

"I'm 10."

"I'm Rose and I'm 12," said the girl, who also shook Christina's hand. Rose's hand was very soft and warm. "We're in room 14. We saw you check in. We're the other two kids who are going to be in your grandmother's mystery book besides you and your brother. Didn't she tell you about us?"

San Antonio "Jail"

Cell 13

23

"No," Christina said, trying to remember whether Mimi had told her and she had just forgotten. Mimi often used local kids from the famous historic sites she wrote about in her mysteries.

"You're so lucky and you're so famous," Rose said. "I feel like I know you from reading your grandmother's mystery books."

"I'm not in those books by choice," Christina protested. "She just volunteers me, if you know what I mean."

"But don't you have fun?" asked Juan. "You get to go a lot of places, and you must be rich and famous by now."

Christina wanted to laugh, but she could see her new co-characters were serious. "Well, it is sort of fun," she admitted. "But I'm not really famous, even though some kids do ask me to sign their milk cartons when I go on school visits with my grandmother. And I'm certainly not rich. I don't get any money from the sale of these books."

"Where's Grant?" Juan asked.

"He's soooooo funny!" Rose said, breaking out into giggles.

"Oh, yeah," said Christina. "My brother's a real hoot."

San Antonio
"Jail"

Cell
13

They all were startled when a voice behind them said, "I'm not an owl—I'm a longhorn. Arrrrggggggh!" He began to poke the other kids in their sides with his finger "horns." The two new kids laughed at his antics, but Christina grumbled, "Knock it off, Grant!"

Grant looked up, puzzled. "Who are they?"

"We're the other two mystery book characters," Juan and Rose said simultaneously.

"Oh, sure," Grant said as if that made perfectly good sense to him. Christina groaned.

"Idea!" said Juan. "Let us show you around this joint while your grandparents get settled in. Our mom and dad already told us we're all having dinner together tonight, so we might as well get to know each other."

Christina didn't really want to get to know anyone right now. She wanted a shower and something cold to drink and to curl up with a good book. But then Rose said the magic word. "I'll show you the—spa!"

Cell
13

The
Spa!

6 WATCHING OUT FOR THE WARDEN

Soon they were relaxing in the spa watching the steam turn the cactus and windows surrounding the hot tub into a drippy, wet, foggy, spooky, fright-night scene. First they put their toes in the hot, bubbly water, then they slipped in and sat on the first step. The warm water felt wonderful as they sipped the icy cold passion fruit punch that Juan had rounded up for them. The next thing they knew, Grant had slid down to the second step and was neck deep in the cauldron. With a giggle, Rose joined him, her dress bubbling up around her like a balloon. Juan plopped down next. And Christina figured, what the heck, she was going to be in trouble for letting Grant get all wet anyway, so she might as well join the party. Splash!

As the four kids sat boiling near to death and slurping big gulps of punch, Juan began talking as if he were telling an old tall tale. His foggy breath and the

Cell
13

The
Spa!

27

steamy room made the story seem eerie, even though Christina knew it was all true.

"It was like this," Juan began. "The Alamo was a mission—you know, like a church. And a fortress. Like a little walled city. During the Texas Revolution of 1836, the Mexican army led by a man named Santa Anna attacked the Alamo. A Texas general named Sam Houston ordered everyone to abandon the fort and destroy it. Instead, the men in the fort decided to defend it. It was sort of a lopsided fight: less than 200 to around 6000. The battle lasted 13 days. They fought to the death."

"Thirteen," Christina muttered to herself. There was that number again, come back to haunt her. Maybe she had **triskaidekaphobia**.

"Whose death?" Grant asked.

"Everyone's death," answered Rose in a sad voice. "All of the men in the Alamo died."

For a moment, the four kids sat quietly, the only sound the double-double-toil-and-trouble boil of the hot tub. Then there really was trouble. A large bushy-headed, blackbearded man stormed out of the fog and yelled at them. "What are you doing in there? This spa is only for adults. Get out! Get out!"

The Spa!

Let's Relax!

Just as quickly as he had appeared, the man disappeared. The kids jumped out of the tub and grabbed towels sitting on a bench nearby.

"Who do you think that was?" Christina asked.

Juan took a guess: "The warden?"

That made the kids giggle as they dried off the best they could. As they tossed the wet towels in a large basket and left the spa, Christina asked Juan, "How do you know all that stuff about the Alamo?"

"Are you kidding?" Juan said. "We go to school in Texas. I think we start studying the Alamo in kindergarten!"

"Is there anything you didn't tell me?" Christina asked, wondering how Mimi was going to make a kid's mystery book out of such a tragic historical event.

Juan grinned. "I left out the ghost."

The Spa!

Let's Relax!

7 FIRE!

The kids got lucky. By the time they got back to their rooms, the adults had all met up and were sitting out on the balcony talking like old friends. Fortunately, the room doors were now unlocked and so the kids slipped into rooms 13 and 14 and changed clothes and dried their hair before their parents could spot—and scold—them.

Christina pranced out onto the balcony with a sweet smile. "We're starving," she said. "When's dinner?"

Immediately, the balcony was filled with the rest of the kids asking the very same question. The word "starving, starving!" filled the cool night air.

"Ok, ok!" the four adults gave up in unison. "We're ready, let's go."

"To the Alamo?" asked Grant.

The adults looked confused.

San Antonio "Jail"

The Adobe Armadillo

"No," said Papa. "To dinner, Grant. You said you were hungry."

Grant rubbed his tummy hard. "I am! But I wanted to see the ghost."

The adults looked at one another in confusion. Papa looked at Grant with suspicion. Behind the adults' backs, the other three kids shook their heads back and forth trying to get Grant to hush up about the ghost.

Grant ignored them, but Mimi saved the day. "A ghost? At the Alamo? Then I want to meet him, too!"

But first, they did go to dinner, which was ok with the kids, since they really, really were hungry after their "sort of" swim in the spa. Christina loved the restaurant, called the Adobe Armadillo. It was very southwestern (Tex-Mex, Juan and Rose's dad called it) with warm brown adobe walls and lots of green prickly cactus. The tabletops were made of colorful ceramic tiles in turquoise, hot pink, and lime designs. The waiters wore large sombreros and silver conch shell belts. The burning candles on the tables smelled like toasted marshmallows.

"I'll have a chimichanga," Christina said. She didn't know what that was, but she liked the sound of it.

The Adobe Armadillo

Let's Eat Tex-Mex!

Alliteration, her English teacher called it. You know, like great green gobs of greasy grimy gopher guts, an example her teacher had actually used.

Continuing around the table, the others ordered tacos, tamales, and a lot of other t-word foods. Papa ordered a steak fajita. The waiter brought out baskets full of warm, toasty tortilla chips and small bowls of bright red, spicy salsa. The kids' drinks were frosty lemonades with little umbrellas stuck in the top.

"Aren't you going to order?" Mimi asked Grant. Christina wasn't sure her brother could read a menu with this many foreign-sounding words.

"Aw, I'll just have an armadillo," Grant said, sitting back in his chair smug and satisfied with his decision.

Everyone laughed.

"You don't really eat armadillo," Juan's dad explained.

"Why not?" asked Grant.

Everyone was quiet.

Juan's dad laughed. "You know, I don't know!"

"Then I'll just have peanuts," Grant said.

"No you won't!" Christina, Mimi, and Papa all said together. The other family looked confused.

Grant folded his little arms tight across his chest

The Adobe
Armadillo

Let's Eat
Tex-Mex!

and looked angry. "Well, then I'll have a piñata."

Juan and Rose laughed. "I told you Grant was soooo funny," Rose said in admiration. "Why don't you have a quesadilla like me," she suggested. "You'll like it!"

Grant looked relieved. "Ok," he agreed, then sat up and started slurping down his big, lemonade drink. "I'll have a piñata for desert."

"Grant, you're a hoot," said Juan.

"I told you," Grant said, "I am not an owl."

"Let's eat!" Papa said, as several waiters soon brought enormous platters of sizzling food all at once.

"Good idea," said Juan and Rose's mother. "I think the natives are getting restless."

Natives? Ghosts? Christina thought maybe she didn't understand the language down here. "Isn't Texas in America?" she asked, not realizing she had said it aloud until Mimi answered her.

"It is," she said. "But it wasn't always!"

As they ate, Juan and Rose's dad, a high school history teacher, told them more of the amazing story of the Alamo. Christina wasn't sure it was great dinner conversation, but it was interesting. As she listened,

The Adobe
Armadillo

Let's Eat
Tex-Mex!

the Alamo grew bigger and bigger in her mind.

"It was a freezing cold night," he said. "It was a Sunday morning, a holy day. The dawn was quiet until Santa Anna gave the order to attack! Bands played the Deguello—a march tune that meant no quarter would be given—it would be a fight to the death."

As Christina munched on tortilla chips and salsa, she remembered that giving "no quarter" was what pirates always said. The thought gave her a chill.

The storyteller went on in a deep, dramatic, actor-sounding voice, waving his arms in the air to help tell his tale. "Suddenly, soldiers threw ladders against all four sides of the old, adobe walls of the fort. They blasted musket balls as they climbed. As they tumbled into the courtyard (those who did not get shot down), the Mexican soldiers and the Alamo defenders fought in hand-to-hand combat."

"That must have been a horrendous sight," Mimi said with a shudder.

The man nodded and went on. "They fought for 13 days and 13 nights, until every man in the Alamo was dead."

"Didn't anyone survive?" Christina asked.

"Only a few. A woman and her child. A servant. A few others," the speaker answered. "Around 1,500 of the

Let's Eat
Tex-Mex!

Alamo
History

Mexicans were killed."

"So, that was the end," Christina said, hoping it really was the end of the sad story.

"Not really," said Papa. "This lost battle gave other Texans a chance to rally their troops. In the next attack, at a place called San Jacinto (Papa pronounced it *yah-sin-toe*), the soldiers cried *Remember the Alamo!* and went on to defeat Santa Anna for all time!"

Everyone was very quiet. There was only the sound of soft munching.

Finally, Grant spoke up. "You mean Davy Crockett got killed, too?" He looked like he might cry.

Papa put his arm around Grant's shoulders. "Yes, he did," he said. "But he was a hero. He fought for what he believed in. He thought freedom was worth dying for. And that's why Texas is part of America today . . . and not part of Mexico."

"Hurrah!" said Mimi, trying to cheer them all up. "Remember the Alamo!"

"Remember the Alamo!" the other adults joined in, clanking their glasses together in a toast.

Suddenly, the valet parking attendant ran into the restaurant. He looked very upset. "The Alamo! The Alamo!" he shouted.

Alamo, shalimo—enough, already, Christina

Let's Eat
Tex-Mex!

Alamo
History?

thought.

"What's wrong?" Papa asked the man.
"The Alamo—it's on fire!"

Let's Eat
Tex-Mex!

Alamo
History

8 THE GHOST

The restaurant turned out to be right around the corner from the Alamo. Christina could not have been more shocked. As a crowd gathered in front of the historic site, Christina craned her neck to look for some enormous building. She was thunderstruck when the famous Alamo turned out to be a small building.

However, it was beautiful against the dark blue early night sky with a full moon behind it. It did look pretty mysterious, even with a bunch of people running around like banshees. She could see why Mimi might think she could make up a good kid's mystery here. But what was the mystery? Not the fire. That turned out to be a trash barrel that someone had tossed a match into.

"False alarm," said Papa, turning to go back to the restaurant. "Thank goodness! Wouldn't want any famous Texas historic sites to go up in smoke."

The Adobe Armadillo

The Alamo!

Papa and the other adults walked on toward the restaurant. The kids lingered behind and the adults didn't seem to notice. The kids stood like statues staring up at the Alamo as the crowds disappeared back to where they had come from.

"I never thought the Alamo would be like . . . like right in the middle of downtown San Antonio," Christina said in amazement.

"Well, it wasn't always in the middle of the city, you know," said Juan. "The missions were built as walled forts on the barren land to protect the people from Indians and Mexicans and anyone else who wanted to bother them."

Christina wondered what it would have been like to live back then. She couldn't imagine living on the lonesome prairie or whatever you called it, in old adobe mud buildings. And worrying about getting attacked, or starving to death, or freezing to death, or getting scalped, or heaven knows what else.

"Today, there is not much of the original Alamo fort and mission left," said Juan. "The building you see here that is so famous in pictures is the shrine. Over there are the soldier's barracks, the hospital, and the powder magazine. These structures, and the gardens and courtyards were all surrounded by an adobe wall with gates."

The Adobe
Armadillo

The
Alamo!

Grant looked up at Juan. In the moonlight, Grant's blond curls glistened like those of an ancient Greek statue carved in white marble. "What's a shrine?"

"It's sort of like a chapel," Rose said. "A place to remember something or someone."

"Like the Battle of the Alamo?" asked Christina.

"Yes," said Rose. "And the people who died there."

"Well, what's a powder magazine?" Grant asked. Christina guessed her brother was imagining make-up or something to read and they didn't quite go together.

"That's where the gunpowder was kept," Juan explained. "You wanted to keep it dry, you know."

"I guess we'd better get back to the restaurant," Rose said, heading off on her own.

"Yeah," said Juan. "Our parents will be looking for us." He followed his sister, and they both disappeared into the darkness.

Grant stood frozen in place. He seemed to be intently watching something or someone.

"What is it, Grant?" Christina asked. She knew they had better skedaddle on back to the restaurant too–before Papa had to come looking for them.

"That trash barrel," Grant said. "I think it's still smoldering."

Christina peered into the foggy darkness. "Are you sure that's not just fog?"

The Alamo!

What Was That?

Grant thrust out his face but kept his feet planted firmly in place. He sniffed. "No. It's smoke. I think we should check it out."

Before Christina could restrain her brother, he galloped off toward the side of the shrine building and the trash barrel, which indeed had smoke signals flowing from it. When Grant refused to turn around, Christina ran after him.

Suddenly, Grant squealed and jumped backwards. The barrel, full of charred wood, fell forward, dumping the logs and embers at his feet. He barely got out of the way before the hot coals splattered on the ground, spattering bright flecks of ash on Grant's feet.

Christina grabbed her brother and snatched him back even further from the smoking wood. "Be careful!" she warned. "You could have gotten burned or even caught your clothes on fire!"

But Grant continued to stare just beyond the barrel.

"Didn't you see?!" he asked her. He seemed very upset.

"The barrel didn't just fall over. Someone pushed it. I saw them!"

"Them who?" asked Christina with skepticism. Surely her brother was imagining things.

The Alamo!

What Was That?

Grant bent over and brushed his knees. Tiny fireflies of embers had landed on his legs and stung. "Ouch! Ouch! Ouch!" he said as he swatted at his knees.

"Who?" Christina demanded. "Who did you see push over the barrel?"

Her brother turned his little face up to hers. "The ghost," he said matter-of-factly. "The Alamo Ghost."

The Alamo!

What Was That?

9 ATTACK OF THE CACTUS

Christina grabbed her brother by the hand and tugged him back toward the safety of the sidewalk and herded him toward the restaurant.

"You know you didn't see any ghost," Christina told him. She didn't believe he had. Surely it was just his active imagination hard at work. Besides, while Mimi loved to put ghosts in her mysteries, she would not like her grandkids tangling with any real ghosts.

"I did too!" Grant insisted. "If you don't believe me, take a look at this." He pulled a piece of charred paper from the waistband of his shorts. "I picked this up from the ground. It had to be stuck on a stick of the wood as a warning. That's why the ghost pushed the barrel over—so I would see the note and get it."

Again, Christina was very **skeptical** of her brother's conclusions. She figured the piece of burnt-edged paper was just trash, an advertisement, a tourist

The Alamo!

The Adobe Armadillo

45

brochure, an old marshmallow package. But when she took the note and read it, she realized it was something else—it was a clue.

The note said:

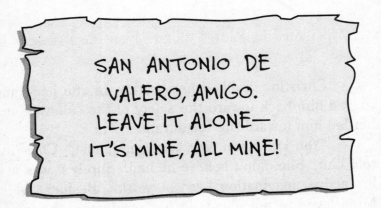

> SAN ANTONIO DE VALERO, AMIGO.
> LEAVE IT ALONE—
> IT'S MINE, ALL MINE!

Just as Christina and Grant began discussing the meaning of the clue, two arms reached out and grabbed the two kids by the scruff of their necks.

"Yow!!!" they both squealed. Christina had just enough time to shove the clue in her pocket where it would be safe until later.

It was Papa. "Where have you two hooligans been?" he demanded. "We're waiting on you to have dessert. Mimi was starting to get worried."

The Alamo!

The Adobe Armadillo

Christina was glad that her grandparents had only been worried and not angry. Still sort of hanging by Papa's big bear paws of hands, they marched on tippy-toe back into the restaurant.

Once inside, Mimi sighed in relief. Juan and Rose gave Grant and Christina a suspicious look as if they had been up to something. But Grant seemed to already have forgotten his mysterious close encounter with a ghost.

"I'll have my piñata, now," he said merrily.

"Grant, a piñata is a papier maché donkey or other animal," Christina explained. "It's covered with colorful pieces of tissue paper. You hit it with a stick until it bursts open and candy falls out."

Grant gave Christina his "So?" look. "Like I said," he said, "dessert!"

The rest of the crowd laughed. Instead, they ate the yummy, sweet, cool flan drizzled in caramel sauce that Mimi had ordered. No one complained.

As the adults had coffee, the kids slipped away and Christina and Grant told Juan and Rose about the happenings at the Alamo.

"Oh, Grant!" Rose said, giving him a hug. Grant squirmed out of her arms.

The Adobe
Armadillo

A Ghost?

"A ghost?" Juan said. He sounded as dubious as Christina had been at first. To convince him, she pulled the piece of burnt paper from her pocket and handed it to him.

He read it slowly, then read it aloud so Rose could hear it.

"I wonder what that means?" Rose said.

"San Antonio de Valero was the original name of the Alamo," Juan said smugly.

Christina was disgusted. It was her job to be the know-it-all! Who did this kid think he was, anyway?

Juan conveniently ignored her frown. "But I don't think a ghost gave you this," he said to Grant.

"Why not?" asked Grant. "You were the one who said there was an Alamo Ghost."

Juan pointed toward a painted bench nestled in a patch of cactus in a small courtyard. "Let's go sit over there and I'll tell you," he said.

In spite of herself, Christina followed them. She and Rose sat on the bench. The boys sat on the pebbled stone walkway in front of them. It was cooler now, and the moonlight was growing dim. Juan began to talk drowsily.

"You know, when I was telling you about the history of the Alamo, you never asked me what happened to all those dead guys," he reminded them.

The Adobe Armadillo

A Ghost?

Grant was hooked. "What did happen to them?" he asked with a frightened quiver in his voice.

Christina tried to look bored, but she listened intently to Juan's answer.

"Some of the dead soldiers were buried in mass graves. Some were thrown into the San Antonio River. And other bodies were incinerated in mounds of earth," Juan explained gravely.

"Incinerated?" Grant asked.

"Burned."

"Oh."

Rose picked up the eerie story. "Supernatural occurrences have been reported in the area of the Alamo for more than a century." She gave her brother a questioning look. He shrugged for her to continue.

"People say they have seen the apparition of a small blonde-haired boy in a window of the Alamo," Rose whispered. "According to legend, he may have been evacuated during the siege of the Alamo . . . and now returns, hoping to find his family."

Neither Grant nor Christina said a word. Juan continued the ghostly tale. "And that's not the only ghost that's been seen around the Alamo. One night, one of the rangers on duty saw a tall man in a long black outfit. It was a hot, summer night—way too hot to wear

The Adobe Armadillo

A Ghost?

a coat. And, the coat was old—from the era of the Alamo battle, not a coat like you might wear today." Juan stopped speaking and just sat there, rocking back and forth in the moonlight.

Finally, Christina found her voice. "And do you believe in these ghosts?" she asked Juan. He looked up at her. "I believe people have seen them."

"Well, I believe I saw one of them tonight," Grant said.

"But what would he want with you, Grant?" Rose asked.

"I don't know," said Grant. "But I'm a little blond kid, too. Maybe he just wanted company."

Christina stretched and yawned. She was tired, and cold from the chilly night air. Goosebumps popped up on her arm like popcorn kernels. "Let's sleep on this," she said, spying their parents coming out of the restaurant and looking all around for their children. "Maybe the clue will make more sense tomorrow."

The other kids nodded and clambered to a standing position. Grant yawned and stretched and bent over to pick up the note from the pavement. As he did he suddenly yelped loudly—"OUCH!"

The Adobe
Armadillo

Be Careful...

Cactus attack!

The other kids almost jumped out of their skins. "What now?" Christina asked.

Grant rubbed his bottom. "I got stuck in the butt by a cactus!" he grumbled.

Be Careful...

Gotcha!

10 ABNORMAL PARANORMAL

The next morning, Mimi and the four "real characters" in her mystery book went on the official tour of the Alamo that she had arranged in advance of their trip. Mimi always liked to get the "deluxe tour," as she called it. Christina knew that meant that they would get to see places and hear stories that the average tourist might not. Sometimes they even got to go through secret passages! Somehow she doubted that they would see any ghosts on this official tour. But maybe they could ask a few ghostly questions, she hoped.

This morning (a clean, bright, blue sky day), there was no sign of the trash barrel, burnt wood, or a ghost. The **curator's** intern giving them the tour was a pretty young woman named Papaya.

"Let's sit here on this adobe wall, and I'll set the scene for you," she suggested. Mimi perched on the low

The
Alamo!

Let's Take
a Tour

mudworks wall and like little birds, the children hopped up along beside her.

"This land was once the land where buffalo herds thundered beside the river," Papaya explained. "Native peoples lived here, perhaps in peace, until the Spanish *conquistadors* came. They believed they would find gold. Their horses and weapons frightened the Indians."

Christina shifted on the wall to get more comfortable. She could just imagine! She listened eagerly, as did the other kids, as Papaya with the pineapple-colored hair and honey voice continued.

"Then the padres–the priests–in gray robes built the Alamo mission. They hoped to protect the people, and to convert them to their religion. Inside the walls, the people lived together in safety. Outside the walls, they grew corn, raised sheep, and hauled water from the river."

Papaya pointed to the tree that spread shade over the wall. "The mission became a fort called the Alamo, the word for the cottonwood tree," Papaya said. "Outside the fort, ranchers raised cattle and farmed in this place that they now called Texas."

"Viva, Texas!" Juan shouted, and Papaya smiled at him.

"But really, this land was still part of the country of Mexico back then," said the intern. "The Mexicans,

Let's Take
a Tour

Practical
Padres

especially General Santa Anna, were very unhappy at the way new people were taking over the land and claiming it for their own.

"In 1835," she continued, "Sarah Seely DeWitt tore up her daughter's wedding gown and stitched it instead into a flag that said COME AND TAKE IT!"

"What did that mean?" Christina asked.

"It was just one step by the frontier people to say that the land was now theirs," said Papaya. "They took over the Alamo."

"And that made the Mexicans mad!" Rose said.

Mimi fanned herself with a pretty green fan she had bought at a gift shop earlier that morning. "And that, you could say, created a powderkeg situation."

"Is that anything like a powder magazine?" Grant asked.

Mimi and the intern laughed. "That's a very good analogy, Grant," Mimi said. Grant didn't know what an analogy was, but he knew a compliment when he heard one. He smiled smugly and wiggled on the wall.

Suddenly, Juan jumped down off the wall and stood in a soldier-like pose with his legs spread out and his hands on his hips. "Enter, Davy Crockett!" he shouted, raising his fist as if he held a rifle in it.

Practical
Padres

Come and
Take It!

"Very good!" Papaya praised him. "You know your Texas history. Davy Crockett did come down from the state of Tennessee to help his old friend James Bowie fight the Mexicans in the battle that was bound to come.

"William Barret Travis was the commander of the Alamo at that time," Papaya went on. "And then ... the fateful night came." Papaya paused for a moment and all the kids—and even Mimi— leaned forward to hear what happened next.

"It is said that he took his sword and drew a line in the sand. He said to the men around him, 'Cross this line if you will stand and fight with me, but know that you will surely die.'"

"Whoa!" said Grant. "Did anyone cross that line?"

"Oh, yes!" said Papaya. "Every man, except one."

"Was he a coward?" Grant asked.

Papaya hesitated. "I do not know," she said. "I'm sure he had his reasons. It was a long time ago. And I was not there," she reminded them with a smile.

"And then what happened?" asked Christina, eager for the story to move along so they could start their tour.

Papaya put her hands out and her palms up. She held them like that as she said, "Legend says that Jim

Come and Take It!

Fight to the Death

Bowie threw silver into the Alamo's wells for safekeeping as they prepared for battle. And then . . . they waited."

Christina gasped. "For what?" she demanded.

"For the battle to begin," Juan said.

"And when it did," Papaya added quickly, "it was a terrible thing! The air was filled with the sound of earsplitting cannon and the lightning sharp crack of rifle fire! The women and children huddled in fear. Their husbands, brothers, and sons fought bravely, but one by one, they were all killed until there was only silence."

When she finished this part of the tale, there was also only silence. Her audience stared at her as they tried to imagine that cold wintery day of March 6, 1836.

At last, Rose spoke. "And then we were Texas?"

"Not quite," said Papaya. "Remember that six weeks later, General Sam Houston caught the Mexican army off guard near the San Jacinto River. Shouting 'Remember the Alamo!' the soldiers won this battle. Just like America many years ago, Texas had gained her independence and become a republic with a government of its own."

Papaya shook the dust off the silver tips of her boots and motioned for them all to follow her.

Fight to the Death

Remember the Alamo!

"In 1845, Texas joined the Union and became the Lone Star State."

"And the Alamo just sat here ever since?" Christina asked, hurrying along to keep up.

Papaya laughed. "Not really. It was used as an army depot, an armory during the War Between the States, a warehouse, and a general store. It pretty much got run down and almost forgotten. Then the Daughters of the Republic came along and helped raise money to save the Alamo."

"That's historic preservation," Christina said, glad she knew something for a change. Her grandmother had told her a lot about how hard and important it was to save neat, old stuff before it went to "rack and ruin" as she put it.

"Yes!" said Papaya. "And that's why today we still remember our Alamo with passion and fondness." With a sweep of her arm, she indicated the historic chapel that they now stood before.

Christina looked up at the warm, sugar cookie color of the beautiful old walls and the worn wooden doors. She figured there was enough history here for a whole semester in school, as well as a whole bunch of tests. But as she spied a dark sleeve in an upstairs window, she remembered that someone might have tried to destroy this special place last night. She

Remember
the Alamo!

The Lone
Star State

wondered if the **curator** knew all about that, but she decided to keep her mouth shut for a change.

When Papaya led them around the corner of the building, Christina arranged to be last in line. As she passed from sunshine into shadow, she felt something flutter behind her. Startled, she spun around in time to see a hand appear from the sleeve in the window and a note flutter to the ground.

Quickly, she picked it up. Sure enough, it was singed around the edges. But before she could read it, Mimi called back to her, "Christina, please keep up, child!"

Christina stuffed the note in her pocket and hurried to catch up with the others. "No problem," she called back to her grandmother. She had no desire to spend any time alone around this creepy, haunted, abnormal, paranormal place!

It's Getting Very Creepy

Who or What Was That?

THE BLACK
SLEEVE
AND THE
BLOND BOY

Christina was dying to tell the others about the new clue. However, first they had to trail the **curator's** intern and Mimi (who was taking notes, talking into her recorder, and making pictures all at the same time!) all around the old mission.

Papaya led them to a large map on a wall. "This is what the Alamo looked like in 1836," she explained.

Christina could see that it had indeed once been a walled city. As a fort, there were officer's quarters, barracks for the soldiers, a hospital, the current chapel, all surrounded by a wall Papaya called a palisade. Christina could not believe how over the years the poor Alamo grounds had been developed until they were surrounded by hotels, and shops, and tourist gift shops, and fast food chains. It was sort of

A New
Clue!

Let's Take
a Tour

sad. Christina didn't feel like just shopping or forgetting the Alamo.

As Mimi started grilling Papaya with a barrage of questions, Christina motioned for the other kids to follow her to a nearby pecan tree where they sat in the shade. Making certain that the adults were not watching them, Christina slipped the note from her pocket to show the others.

"Wow!" said Grant. "Where did that come from?"

"When we were near the front of the Alamo chapel, I saw a black sleeve in the window. As I passed by, this note fluttered to the ground," Christina explained. Juan looked at her strangely. "Are you making this up? Is this something the grandkids of a mystery writer do for fun? Are you teasing us?"

"No!" Christina insisted. "You think I want to be the recipient of creepy old clues that don't make any sense?" She shoved the note at the boy. "Here, you take it. I don't know what it means anyway."

Juan picked up the now dusty note and read aloud:

A New Clue!

Let's Take a Tour

What do you make of this?

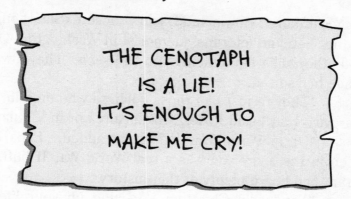

THE CENOTAPH
IS A LIE!
IT'S ENOUGH TO
MAKE ME CRY!

"A cenotaph sounds like a tombstone," Grant offered.

"Not bad, Grant," said Juan in admiration. "That's actually pretty close. It's sort of like a tomb, only the bodies are somewhere else. In this case, it's a memorial to the defenders of the Alamo who died." And then he surprised them all by saying, "C'mon, I'll show you!"

Mimi and Papaya were still gabbing away and paid no attention when the kids headed to the area of the grounds where the large stone cenotaph stood.

"See," said Juan, with reverence. "Here are the names of the men who died defending freedom." Christina marveled at the long list of names. Of course, she did not know most of them, but she recognized the

Let's Take
a Tour

The Alamo
Cenotaph

names of James Bowie and David Crockett. She thought of the Vietnam Veterans' memorial in Washington, D.C. and other such monuments she had seen. They always made her so sad.

"They're just like those soldiers who died in the war with Iraq," said Rose. "Or in Korea or in Vietnam."

"Or in World War II," Grant added. Papa had been in the army and was a real World War II buff, so Grant had heard plenty of that history.

"Yes," said Christina. "Giving up your life to protect your country is a longstanding American tradition, there's no doubt."

"It makes you feel really patriotic to be here," Rose said.

"Hey," said Grant, "they don't sell those red, white and blue popsicles around here anywhere, do they?"

Juan laughed. "As a matter of fact, they do. Just across the street. Let's go!"

"Hey!" Christina called after the others as they sped off without her. "What about the mystery? The clue? The ghost?"

Juan spun around and frowned at her. "Look!" he said, indicating the entire Alamo plaza area. "Do you see any mystery? Do you see any ghost?"

Let's Take a Tour

The Alamo Cenotaph

Christina had to admit that she did not. But it was broad daylight, after all. However, the clue—a second one, at that—was real. And even though she didn't see it, so was the black sleeve still billowing out of the upstairs corner window.

Let's Take
a Tour

The Alamo
Cenotaph

12 THE CENOTAPH

As they slurped the cold, fruity popsicles, the names on the Cenotaph haunted Christina. What, she wondered, could someone wanting the Alamo to be theirs and the names on the memorial have to do with one another? What was the "lie"? Was the Alamo in any real danger? If so, why were a bunch of kids getting the clues?

Christina had lots of questions but no answers, and so it was easy to be persuaded to go off with the other kids on a tour of downtown San Antonio. Mimi gave them permission, as long as they stayed together and met her at "Noon, sharp!" at the River Walk Cafe.

The kids **synchronized** the Carole Marsh Mystery watches that Papa had given them to keep time. He hated for anyone to be late for any appointment. He said it was rude.

The Alamo
Cenotaph

Downtown
San Antonio

Juan and Rose just about wore Christina and Grant out on their "short" walking tour of downtown San Antonio. First they went to La Villita, the original Indian village of Yuanaguana that eventually became San Antonio.

"What does Yanaguana mean?" Grant asked. Rose laughed and told him. "Drunken old man going home at night. It was named after the twisting, winding San Antonio River."

"What happened to the Indians?" Grant asked next.

Christina sighed. "The same thing that happened to a lot of the early native Americans," she said. "They died from things like measly old measles because they didn't have any immunity to the white man's diseases."

"And," added Juan, "they were often killed for their land. Even if they went to live in the missions, they were forced to work hard and farm like slaves. Before long, there just weren't any of the original inhabitants left here."

The kids walked on, silent in thought. Christina pondered how so much of history was about war. Even today, she thought. When would it ever end?

They walked fast past the Menger Hotel after Juan assured them it was haunted. "I'm just not in the

Downtown
San Antonio

San Antonio
River

Peeking around the corner

mood for any more ghosts," Christina insisted. "I think we've already met two ghosts too many in this city."

Grant was really excited when the famous Alamodome came into view. And then he and Christina gasped when they spotted the tall Tower of the Americas that looked like a big spike sticking up into the sky.

"That was the site of the 1968 Hemisfair," Rose said.

"I'd really like to go up to its observation tower," Grant said hopefully.

"Maybe later," Christina said. "We've got to meet Mimi soon," she added, checking her watch. "Hey, Juan, where is the River Walk?"

Juan just smiled and turned the corner. When she followed him, Christina gasped at the beautiful sight before her. The San Antonio River wove its way through the center of downtown. It was a pretty little waterway with sidewalk cafes, shops, and tiny arched bridges connecting one side with the other. There were trees and flowers everywhere. It looked so cool and inviting, Christina thought she could sit down on the river's bank and stay there forever.

"Hey, look!" Grant cried as a small boat floated into view. It was filled with tourists who looked happy

Downtown
San Antonio

San Antonio
River

and barely listening to the oarsman guide as he chirped out his spiel about the surrounding scenery. "Can we go for a ride?"

"No, Grant," Christina insisted. "It's time to meet Mimi and there's the restaurant . . . right over there." She pointed across the river so instead of complaining, Grant took off running up and over the little bridge. He waved to them from the top.

Mimi waited for them on the other side. She was already sitting at one of the little cafe tables scattered everywhere along the River Walk. She had spread out her research and was tapping away happily on her laptop computer beneath a colorful umbrella when she spied the kids and waved them over.

"Over here!" she called. "I've already ordered lunch," she said. The kids looked disappointed until she told them it was *chile con carne*, grilled cheese sandwiches, and chocolate milkshakes.

It was only then that Christina realized she was starving. Mimi moved her things to an extra chair and the kids sat down.

"How's the book going?" Christina asked. She always liked to proofread the first draft and catch all Mimi's mistakes.

Her grandmother shook her head. "Not too good," she admitted. "Papaya gave me lots of

The River
Walk

Let's Eat
Lunch!

information, but I just can't seem to get into the story. Seems like I need a ghost or two or something." Grant opened his mouth to say something, and since Christina had a pretty good idea of what it was, she immediately stuffed a tortilla chip full of salsa into it.

"*Grubblebrmg,*" Grant said.

"What, Grant?" Mimi asked.

"He says he knows he's not supposed to eat with his mouth full," Christina translated. Grant gave her a mean look.

Mimi ignored the kids and seemed to be thinking out loud to herself. "I learned that termites are eating away at the Alamo," she said. "And that someone has been vandalizing the area. Remember that trash barrel fire last night? It was set on purpose," she added.

"*Grumbgrb,*" Grant said.

"Hush!" Christina hissed in his ear.

"That's not the only thing that's happened," Mimi went on. "There have been historical items stolen and graffiti written in Spanish on some of the walls. Papaya seemed to be really worried that the problem was getting worse and that something really bad could happen to the Alamo—which would be a shame after all the trouble it took to restore it."

The River Walk

Let's Eat Lunch!

Before the kids could respond, a waitress in a colorful Mexican skirt and a white peasant blouse brought their lunch. Mimi stared up at the blue sky and white clouds thinking mysterious thoughts while the kids began to gobble down the delicious food.

Christina was so busy eating that she never noticed the long, black sleeve of the diner sitting at the table right behind her.

The River
Walk

Let's Eat
Lunch!

13 KING OF THE WILD FRONTIER

When they finished eating, Mimi yawned and said she was headed back to the hotel. She gathered up her stuff and left. She had already paid the bill and told Christina to wait for the receipt and bring it with her when she came back to the hotel. She gave the kids permission to sightsee and shop for souvenirs for another hour and then to return to the hotel before Papa got back from his golf game. "We have a busy evening tonight," she promised mysteriously.

As the kids finished slurping their milkshakes, Grant asked, "What was Davy Crockett doing in Texas?"

"I know the answer to that!" Rose volunteered. "I had to do a book report on him for school. He was born in Tennessee. His grandparents were killed by Indians before he was born. When he was just 12 years

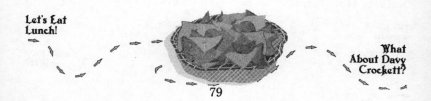

Let's Eat Lunch!

What About Davy Crockett?

79

old, his father hired him out to drive cattle 300 miles to Virginia!"

"Didn't he have to go to school?" asked Grant. Rose shook her head. "He didn't even start school till he was 13, and then he didn't like it. He often played hooky and even ran away and went on another cattle drive."

"Did he ever come back?" Grant asked.

"Not until more than two years later!" Rose said. "In his whole lifetime, he only went to school a total of 100 days."

"What did he do next?" Christina asked.

"He got married, had kids, and served as a Congressman," Rose said. "But what he liked best was telling stories. He told people that he had killed 105 black bears. He usually told these tall tales while wearing his coonskin cap and toting his rifle, which he called Brown Bess."

"Tell them how he got to Texas," Juan said.

"Oh, yeah," said Rose. "He decided to move to Texas and got here just in time to fight at the battle of the Alamo. It's believed he was captured and later killed. And, of course, he became a famous legend in American history."

"Yeah!" said Grant, standing on his chair. "As king of the wild frontier!" Grant shoved the tortilla chip

Let's Eat Lunch!

What About Davy Crockett?

basket on his head like a coonskin cap and brandished a butter knife like a rifle.

It would have been cute and funny, Christina thought, except—not surprisingly—her brother tumbled backwards and fell onto the brick floor. He screamed bloody murder but was instantly helped up a long arm covered in a black sleeve.

Christina was so focused on her brother that she did not even notice. "Grant!" she cried. "Are you ok?"

Juan and Rose helped Grant back up into his chair. The basket still sat cockeyed on top of his head, hanging down over one eye. "I think so," he said. "Maybe next time I fall, I can fall in the river and it won't hurt so much."

"No more falling!" Christina warned him. She picked up the receipt Mimi had asked her to bring, but when she looked down to check it, she saw that it was not a copy of the bill but a new clue!

"Wow!" said Juan, realizing what it was. "Read it." Christina spread the clue out on the table.

What About Davy Crockett?

A New Clue!

A New Clue! from Who?

14 A HELPING HAND

"That's Spanish," said Grant. "Uh, oh, amigo, and all that jazz."

"I know that," Christina said. "But what is the Paseo del Rio?"

Rose looked over Christina's shoulder and motioned to indicate the waterway. "It's the River Walk," she said.

All the way back to the hotel, Christina pondered who had put the clue on their table and what it meant. Why give it to her? Why say they would see her at the river—she wasn't even going to be on the river, as far as she knew. And if she was there, what did they want with her—or all the kids for that matter—and what would they do if they found them? It was still a little while before they needed to get back and when Grant—who

The River
Walk

Downtown
San Antonio

felt better after his bump on the head—spied a Circus Museum, he was determined to go inside.

"Can we go?" he begged. Grant loved the circus almost more than anything else.

"You know it's not a circus, don't you?" Christina asked. "It's a museum of circus stuff," she explained to him.

"I know what a museum is," he grumbled, getting in line to get a ticket.

The others followed him and once inside, they were glad they had come. The delightful museum was filled with all kinds of circus memorabilia. Antique circus posters filled one entire wall. They saw Tom Thumb's tiny carriage. But the best thing was a model of a three-ring circus. Christina loved the incredible details and wondered how long it had taken someone to put the exhibit together—probably years and years, she guessed.

On their way out, they spied several of those funhouse mirrors that make you look **FAT**, SKINNY, or Ǝpᴉsd∩ DOWN. Naturally, each of them had to parade before every mirror, giggling while they helped make themselves look as funny as possible.

Juan and Rose were the first to head out the door, then Christina, until she heard Grant scream. She flew back inside.

Downtown
San Antonio

Circus
Museum

"Are you hurt?" she asked. "Did you fall again?"

"No, no!" Grant insisted. He pointed to the mirror. "I saw the ghost."

"The black sleeve ghost?" his sister asked.

"No, no, no!" Grant said. "The little boy ghost . . . the one that looks like me."

Christina stared into the mirror. She saw nothing but their reflections. Her brother must just be seeing things because of the bump on his head, she thought. Surely that's all it was. She put her arm around Grant's shoulders and gently herded him outside.

"C'mon, Grant," she said. "It's time to go home now."

Home, of course, was still Cell 13. When they got there, Mimi and Papa insisted that the kids take a *siesta*.

"We're too old for a nap," Christina protested.

"But you're never too old to rest," Papa insisted, with a big yawn. "Trust me!"

Juan and Rose went to their room and Christina and Grant plopped down on the twin beds with the black and white striped bedspreads and started to read.

Circus
Museum

San Antonio
"Jail"

Christina picked up a book from the bedside table about Sam Houston.

"Hey, listen to this," Christina told her drowsy brother. "Sam Houston was born in Virginia but when his father died, he moved to Tennessee."

"Just like Davy," Grant mumbled.

"Yes," said Christina. "And he only went to school for one year."

"I knew I should have been born in the frontier days," Grant said with a sigh.

Christina kept reading, sharing interesting tidbits with her sleepy brother. "He ran away to live with a Cherokee Indian tribe! He enlisted in the army and was wounded at the Battle of Horseshoe Bend. He was friends with General Stonewall Jackson! He taught himself law and became governor of Tennessee! Then he came to Mexico and was named head of the Texas army. He became the president of the new republic of Texas. Did you know that?"

When Christina turned around to see why her brother did not answer, she saw that he had fallen fast asleep. In spite of herself, Christina slept, too. When she woke up, she tiptoed out of the room and went to find Juan. He was on the balcony reading.

"Boo!" Christina said, coming up behind him and nearly scaring him to death.

San Antonio
"Jail"

Cell
13

"Hey, knock it off!" Juan said, swatting at Christina with his book.

"Think you saw a ghost?" Christina teased him.

"Don't be so surprised," Juan said. "It could happen, you know."

Christina sat down beside him. "Yeah," she said solemnly. "I know." She got quiet a moment, watching the deep red southwestern sun sink into the dark blue horizon that seemed so far away. "You know, I think I have a bright idea," she said.

"What's that?" Juan asked, putting his book away.

"I think we should go to the Alamo tonight after dark and confront these ghosts or whatever they are and get to the bottom of this mystery," Christina said bravely. "I'm sick and tired of looking over my shoulder waiting for something—or someone—to happen."

"Good plan!" said Juan. "I'm in."

"In what?" his dad asked, coming out onto the balcony all dressed for dinner.

Juan squirmed in his chair. "Uh, in the mood for a big dinner," he said.

"Well, let's go, amigos!" said Papa. Christina noted that her grandfather wore his dress jeans, a stiffly

Cell
13

Cell
13

starched blue denim shirt, and a handsome turquoise bola instead of a tie. With his cowboy hat and boots, he looked like a real Texan.

When Mimi joined them on the balcony, Papa whistled and said, "Oolala, lady!"

Christina thought Mimi looked beautiful in her new, chili-pepper-red broomstraw skirt and white off-the-shoulder peasant blouse. She wore a bright yellow flower in her hair.

"I'm dying to eat," she said.

Suddenly Grant wandered out onto the porch. His hair looked like a hundred cows had licked it. "I slept like a dead boy," he said with a yawn.

As they headed for dinner, Christina wished people would quit using the d-word.

Cell 13

The River Walk

15 PASEO DEL RIO

Christina was stunned when they went to dinner. The *hacienda*-style restaurant was on the River Walk. But this was not the same Paseo del Rio she had seen earlier today. At night, a million white and colored lights twinkling in the trees and reflecting in the water turned the entire area into a fairyland.

"It's beautiful!" she said.

Rose put her arm around Christina's waist. "You should see it at Christmas time," she said.

Christina could just imagine. But tonight was beautiful enough for her. The smells of roasting meat, cinnamony spices, burning candles, and lemony flowers only added to the wonderful feel of the cool night air. The night was also filled with the sounds of *mariachi* bands playing lively Mexican music up and down the River Walk.

The River Walk

Let's Eat Dinner!

89

As they ate dinner, Mimi reported on her day of writing. "I'm just stumped for ideas," she confessed. "Maybe I'll just have to give up writing mysteries," she added sadly, although Christina could tell she was just teasing them and looking for a little sympathy.

"Oh, no!" the children shouted together.

"We'll help you," Christina said. "Don't we always?"

Mimi laughed. "Yes," she admitted, "but usually by getting in trouble."

"Yeah," said Grant. "And then you put it your mystery book and that's ok, right?"

"Wrong!" said Papa and everyone laughed.

After dinner, the adults drank steaming cups of hot coffee and danced to the music on the slick tile dance floor. They didn't notice that the kids—who had asked to "go to the bathroom"—had never returned.

Outside the restaurant, Christina egged the others on. "Now is our chance," she said.

"To do what?" asked Grant.

"To explore the Alamo on our own," Christina said.

"No way," said Grant. "Too scary."

"Too bad," said Christina, hurrying them all to

Let's Eat
Dinner

To the
River!

the side of the river as one of the little boats approached the dock.

With Juan's help, she got Rose and Grant aboard, then she and Juan hopped on.

"Hey, this is fun," said Grant, who loved boats and any kind of water.

"It's my favorite thing to do in San Antonio," Rose agreed.

Juan dangled his arm over the side of the boat, his fingertips threading through the cool water. "Aw, it's ok," he said, but Christina could tell he was enjoying it. As for herself, she thought it was very romantic.

For awhile, the boat was crowded with tourists. The boat followed the narrow, winding waterway. Beneath the overhanging trees, dark shadows loomed, the foliage so thick that the little twinkly lights could not penetrate the darkness. An oarsman in a long black outfit kept the boat moving with the long sweep of black-sleeved arms.

As they went on, tourists hopped out of the boat at various stops to go to restaurants, shops, or back to their hotel rooms. Juan sat in the front of the boat, watching in the darkness for their stop. Rose sat behind him and Christina behind her, each on their own bench as the boat emptied out. Grant stretched out on

To the River!

Now. To The Alamo!

his tummy on the back of the boat as if he might fall asleep again.

In a few more turns, the waterway entered a darker stretch with few buildings and even fewer lights. It felt like they might be getting lost. Christina was getting worried.

"Shouldn't we get out soon?" she asked Juan.

Juan looked concerned, too. "Yeah. Right here at this stop," he demanded with an urgent tone in his voice. As the boat bumped against the side of the river bank, he turned to help Rose out. Christina turned to help Grant, but—Grant was gone!

To the River!

Now, To The Alamo!

16 FEAR AND TREMBLING

Christina screamed. She jumped right out of the boat. The oarsman was nowhere to be seen. Neither was Grant.

"What's wrong?" asked Juan.

"Grant's disappeared," Rose said as she watched Christina look all around the side and back of the boat, which was starting to drift away.

"Grant!" Christina cried.

"Grant! Grant! Where are you? Answer us!" they all hollered into the darkness. The only answer was the *plop plop plop* of water sloshing against the side of the river bank.

Christina thought she would cry. What if her brother had drowned? Even though he was a good swimmer, what if he had fallen overboard while asleep? She didn't even want to think about it.

Now, To The Alamo!

Where is Grant?

"C'mon," Juan urged her, tugging her by the arm. "Your brother is obviously not here. And we can't go back—there's not a boat in sight. Maybe he hopped out when you weren't looking. To play a trick, you know. Like a practical joke."

Christina held back her tears. "It wouldn't be a very funny joke," she said, her voice trembling.

"No, it wouldn't," said Rose, who looked like she might cry as well.

Juan looked like he couldn't take it if they both broke down in tears. "C'mon," he insisted once more. "Let's go to the Alamo like we planned. It's possible Grant is there waiting for us. The little varmint!"

That made the girls laugh. Brushing tears from her eyes, Christina nodded in agreement, and they all raced across the nearest bridge and up the steps to the street. They ran toward the Alamo Plaza.

By this time of night, the streets had cleared out. As they approached the Alamo, Christina groaned. She could immediately tell by how dark it was that the historic site had already closed for the night.

"But isn't that good?" Juan asked. "Now we won't be disturbed while we go on our ghost walk."

Christina put her hands on her hips and stuck out her lip. "You don't have to put it that way,

Where is Grant?

Is He At The Alamo?

Don't worry, Christina!

you know," she said, nodding toward Rose, who looked scared.

Juan nodded back. "Right! This is just an adventure. If we stick together, we'll be all right."

So, together, they all walked as **nonchalantly** as they could along the palisade wall until they found a shadowy, overgrown place where they could climb over. One by one, they disappeared over the wall onto the haunted grounds of the Alamo.

Is He At The Alamo?

Let's Look!!

17 GHOST WALK

"What now?" Juan asked. "This is your party," he said to Christina. They could barely see one another in the darkness.

"Let's stop and recap," Christina said, "before we get started. Maybe we can deduce some meaning from the clues we have."

"Ok," said Juan. "One: We think we've seen two ghosts. A blond-headed boy and someone wearing a black gown with a billowy black sleeve."

"Two," Christina said, "we have clues about a San Antonio de Valero, a Cenotaph, and a river threat."

"We have a missing boy," Rose reminded them.

"Don't remind me," said Christina, knowing she should not be here in the dark, creepy Alamo compound, but instead running back to Mimi and Papa for help in finding Grant.

Let's Look!!

Where Do
We Start?

"And," added Juan, "we have all those bad things happening at the Alamo your grandmother talked about."

"And," said a small voice from the darkness beyond, "we have hungry termites."

"Grant?" Christina screamed. "GRANT?! Is that you? I'm gonna get you, boy!"

Grant giggled as he walked out of the darkness like a small ghost himself. "Ok, ok, forget about the termites," he said.

"Termite, shermite, where were you?" his sister demanded.

Grant shrugged his tiny shoulders. "I'm always last 'cause I'm the youngest," he said. "I just wanted to get here first and surprise you."

Christina reached out and shook him by the shoulders, gently, but she meant it. "You scared us to death." There was that word again.

"Sorry," Grant said sincerely.

But before they could continue the discussion, they heard a rustling in the area of the old barracks building.

"Rats?" Juan whispered.

"Ghosts?" suggested Rose.

"The wind?" Grant said hopefully.

Grant!

What Was That?

"Bad news," insisted Christina. "We are obviously not alone in the Alamo tonight."

"Come on," she said, and led them off into the darkness toward the spooky sound they had heard.

18 DRATS, RATS!

Christina had no plan. She sort of had the Alamo compound layout clear in her head and all she knew was to scout out each building, each area, until she found what she had come for. She wasn't sure what that was exactly, though.

The four kids tiptoed so silently in the soft dirt that they could hear one another's breath. As gently and quietly as he could, Juan pulled open the door to the barracks. The old wood was as soft as fur. The door was heavy. The iron latches felt like cold skeleton bones against the palm of his sweating hand.

"Shhh," Christina reminded them as they went inside. It was pitch black. They had to feel their way along the ancient walls. Christina did not want to think about rats. Even meeting up with a ghost would be more welcome, she thought–then wished she had not thought that at all.

Rats?!

To The
Barracks

They tried to walk without touching anything, just trying to see ahead even just a little bit. But every now and then, Christina's hand accidentally landed on an artifact. One was hard and round and cold. She hoped that it was a helmet and not a skull.

Pretty soon, they saw a little light, but it was just when Juan opened the door at the other end of the barracks and they all slipped out.

"Nothing there," he said.

Christina did not want them to lose the little bravery they had. "Let's keep going," she said, leading the way toward the old hospital building.

Once inside, she really didn't want to think about what had gone on in here a long time ago. Blood and guts and amputations and old medical tools that were more like torture chamber stuff just weren't her thing. As it turned out, it didn't matter. This building, too, was empty. Or at least no ghost was showing its face tonight. They went back out into the courtyard. The only place left to go was the place Christina feared most—the old Alamo chapel. As they passed through the darkest part of the courtyard, things seemed to be going smoothly when Grant yelped.

Christina's blood froze in her veins. "What's wrong now, Grant?" she pleaded.

The Barracks   The Hospital

"Cactus. Just cactus," the boy said. "It loves my bottom."

Rose giggled and Juan shushed her. They marched on.

Christina did not really want to be the first one to go into the ancient and historical building that had been the site of so much pain and death. And heroism, she tried to remember. But no one else offered, so she went in first. She thought the others had followed. She did not realize that Juan had said, "Let's stand guard out here," and the other kids gladly froze in place.

Not knowing this, Christina—more or less (mostly less) bravely—began her search in the chapel. It was cooler in here. Very creepy feeling. And there were noises. Not rustling like mice. Just sounds. Eerie, creepy sounds and she could not pinpoint what they were or where they came from.

As Christina made her way around the old walls of the room, she wondered who would want to hurt the Alamo and if there really were such things as ghosts. Soon she realized that she had reached the far wall and found nothing. She didn't know whether to be disappointed or relieved.

Turning, she realized two things. One, was that she was alone; the kids had abandoned her. Probably

Watch Out...

Gotcha!

gone back to the restaurant, she thought. Cowards!
Two, was that there was an upstairs loft to this place
and that someone in a long black dress with long black
sleeves was coming down the ladder toward her.

Where Is
Everybody?

Uh Oh!

19 NIGHT OF THE DEAD

Christina froze in place. You should be running, she tried to tell herself, but her feet would not move. She opened her mouth to scream, but before she could, a large, rough hand wrapped itself over her mouth and a gruff voice said, "I wouldn't do that, *senorita*."

With a grip on her arm and the hand still over her mouth, the black dress billowing against the back of her legs, the person or thing, marched Christina slowly toward the door.

Christina squirmed, but she could not get away. With a dusty, booted foot, her captor opened the door and marched her out into the darkness. Only suddenly, there was not darkness!

All at once, the security lights all around the Alamo grounds burst on like blazing fireworks! Blue lights from police cars began to swirl and their sirens spewed a deafening shriek. The other kids were there

Uh Oh!

It's Got Me!

and ran toward Christina and grabbed her away. Mimi and Papa were there with their mouths gaping wide open. Juan and Rose's parents looked angry. But most angry of all was the Alamo's intern. She stalked right up to the black-dressed creature and said, "Gotcha!"

Mimi and Papa came running up and grabbed Grant and Christina and hugged them hard.

"What were you thinking?" Mimi asked.

"How did you know we were here?" Grant asked back.

"We got worried about you when you didn't come back from the bathroom—*for an hour*!" Juan and Rose's dad groused.

"We were trying to save the Alamo," Grant said.

"From what?" Papa demanded.

"From him," Christina said, pointing at the black draped figure which just stood there, its head hung down in a long, black hood. Or it, Christina thought to herself, knowing she would not be surprised if the black cloak suddenly fell to the ground, leaving nothing behind. She just hoped all these adults were ready for that! Because she sure wasn't!!

Finally, Papa got the police to turn off the sirens out and the floodlights. He walked toward the

Trying To Save
The Alamo

Exlain This!

black-hooded figure. "You've got some explaining to do!" Papa said. He swooped the hood off and everyone gasped.

"It's a woman!" Rose cried.

"Actually, she's just a girl," said Mimi.

Everyone was so surprised that they stepped back a little. She doesn't look scary at all, Christina thought. Surely there's a mistake. How could she be behind all the bad goings-on at the Alamo? Why would she want to harm it? Or them?

Those were all good questions, and Papa and Papaya stood their ground and began to ask the girl to explain herself.

"Who are you?" Papaya demanded.

The girl sighed. "I'm Angelina. I am a descendant of one of the defenders of the Alamo."

"Who?" Papa demanded.

The girl hung her head. "The one . . ." she began, then faltered. "The one who would not fight."

Everyone stared at her.

"Oh!" said Juan suddenly. "The one who would not cross the line drawn in the sand. Everyone else agreed to fight and die. That one man refused."

"He had a good reason!" the girl swore.

"What was that reason?" Mimi asked gently.

Trying To Save
The Alamo

Exlain This!

"To save the woman who would one day give birth to my great, great, great-grandmother. And to save a small boy," the girl said in a weak, but proud voice.

"And how do you know this?" Papaya asked, perplexed.

The girl removed the black cloak and let it fall to the ground. She was wearing well-worn western jeans and a tattered sweater. "The story has been handed down in an oral tradition by our family since the time of San Antonio de Valero—the Alamo," she said. "My family was ruined by the shame, but no one ever knew that my ancestor was truly a hero. We always believed that if his name was on the Cenotaph, he would regain respect and our family would regain its fortune."

Now Papaya really was confused. "Fortune?"

The girl lifted her head proudly now. "The silver," she said. "The silver that was tossed into the wells. Much of that silver was ours from my ancestor's cattle business."

Christina looked at Juan. She recalled that Papaya had mentioned something about silver when they were on the tour. So was that a legend or true? If it was true, then why had they been looking for ghosts when they could have been searching for silver?!

Trying To Save
The Alamo

Exlain This!

"Why did you pester these kids?" Papa asked.

The girl smiled at the children. "I meant them no harm," she said. "But they were nosy, coming too close. I thought they might find me out before I finished my mission."

"And what mission is that, miss?" a policeman said, stepping forward with a pair of handcuffs. "To find the silver and prove that the story I tell is true so that history can be rewritten and my ancestor's name added to the Cenotaph," the girl answered.

Without another word, the police officer came forward, read the girl her rights, and gently guided her to the police car.

As the car drove off, the others stood silently.

"Is this story true?" Mimi asked Papaya.

Papaya shrugged her shoulders. "If so, it is a new one to me," she said. "I believe in revisionist history, but only if it is true. This girl will have a lot of work to prove her tall tale."

"Speaking of tall tales," said Mimi. "I know some kids who have some explaining to do . . . or *they* just might get locked up in a cell!"

The Alamo

San Antonio "Jail"

20 IN TROUBLE AGAIN

The kids were marched around the corner and back to the hotel and good old Cell 13. The four of them plunked down on the king-size bed where they were then interrogated by the four adults.

"You *said* the Alamo was in trouble," Christina protested.

"And so *you* thought you would save it?" Mimi asked, incredulous.

"We couldn't help it that we saw a ghost that night the trash barrel caught on fire," Grant said.

"A ghost wearing a black dress?" Papa asked.

"No," Grant said, "A little boy ghost . . . a little boy ghost that looks like me."

Christina wished Grant would keep his mouth shut about that. No use confusing the issue and getting them in more trouble. She tried to change the subject.

San Antonio
"Jail"

Cell
13

113

"We just thought we could figure out the clues," she said. "You know how much we like mysteries."

Mimi laughed. "Well, I guess I have to take the blame for that," she said. She had given her grandchildren mystery books to read ever since they started reading. She said they made a good bridge between READ ING CHOP PY LIKE THIS and reading like a *real* reader.

"Well, ok," Juan and Rose's mom said reluctantly. "I guess that's enough interrogation for tonight. You kids are really pretty dirty. I think you need to get cleaned up and get to bed." The other adults nodded. They paraded out onto the patio to have their coffee—and probably discuss how hard it was to raise kids, Christina imagined!

"Heeyyyyy," said Juan. "I know how we can do just that." He jumped off the bed.

Christina and the others caught his drift right away. "SPA!" they all said together. Then, afraid their parents might have heard them, they said it again softly, "spa." And off they went!

The hot, steamy water felt just as good as it had the first time they had enjoyed the hot tub in the jungle of exotic plants.

Cell
13
→

The
Spa!

"We weren't really that dirty," Christina said, slipping down into the hot water. She wore her new bathing suit.

"Yeah," said Rose, "it was just Alamo dust on our clothes and shoes, that's all." She wore shorts and a tee shirt.

Juan had on a pair of cutoff jeans. He slipped into the water with a big, "AHHHHHHH!"

Grant stood on the side of the hot tub wrapped in a thick towel. He looked embarrassed.

"Come on in, Grant," Christina said. "You're probably the dirtiest of all."

"Am not!" said Grant angrily. "But I forgot my bathing suit," he admitted shyly.

"Well, what have you got on under that towel—your birthday suit!" Juan teased him.

"No!" said Grant and stamped his foot. "My underwear."

The girls giggled. Grant looked like he might cry. Christina knew he did not like to be left out of anything. "It's ok, Grant," she said. "It's just underwear. We won't peek. Come on in." She covered her eyes and Rose did the same. Juan just smirked at the small boy. Grant threw off the towel and dashed for the tub. But before he could get in, he started hollering.

The Spa!

Let's Relax!

"What is it?" Christina said, peeking between her fingers.

Grant rubbed the back of his tiny underpants. "CACTUS!!!!!!" he squealed and cannonballed into the hot water.

21 DON'T FORGET TO REMEMBER THE ALAMO

The next day, it was time to say "Adiós!" and go home. Christina hated to leave. She felt like she was just getting to know a little of Texas history. There were other beautiful historic missions on the river she would like to visit. And to go up in the Hemisphere. And the San Antonio library. And the Japanese tea garden. And the zoo. But she knew Mimi always said you couldn't do everything when you traveled and that's why you had to come back. Christina hoped she could come back to San Antonio one day.

Before they could head to the airport, they had to "pay their bail," as the hotel put it and return their cell keys. *"Gracias,"* the housekeeper in the black and white striped dress said to Papa, as he gave her a tip on the way out.

"You kids sure look clean this morning," Papa said as he herded them downstairs to breakfast.

San Antonio
"Jail"

Breakfast!

117

"Uh, yeah," said Christina. "We took a good hot bath."

At breakfast, they had *huevos rancheros*, which turned out to be scrambled eggs with salsa.

"Mimi," Christina said, "you sure are quiet this morning. Is something wrong?"

Mimi sighed. "Oh, I'm just worried about that girl. I hope she will get some help. She really didn't do anything so terrible, you know. I have to admire anyone who wants the true story of history to be told. That's not so easy, you know."

Papa nodded in agreement. "And how's your mystery coming along?" he asked, trying to cheer her up.

Mimi sighed even deeper. "Oh, with all the commotion, I really didn't get much writing done. I really wanted to write a really cool mystery with kids all in trouble and ghosts and stuff like that. Now I don't know what I'm going to write about."

"MIMI!" Grant and Christina cried together.

Mimi looked up and smiled and her grandchildren realized that she had been teasing them all along.

"Hey, where are Juan and Rose and their parents this morning?" asked Papa.

San Antonio "Jail"

Breakfast!

"They phoned earlier," Mimi said. "They had to catch an earlier flight." She reached in her purse. "But they gave me this postcard to give to you," she said, handing the River Walk postcard to Christina.

Christina and Grant huddled over it together. Grant was reading pretty well these days. He read aloud.

Grant and Christina,

Never forget to remember the Alamo! And never forget us.

Juan and Rose

PS: Grant, stay away from the cactus!

To:
Grant & Christina

Everyone laughed. Christina thought how much fun it was to make new friends—*amigos*. She wished she'd had a chance to say goodbye in person. Maybe she could send them a postcard.

"Grant, you're reading really well these days," Mimi said in admiration.

San Antonio "Jail"

Breakfast!

"I know!" said Grant proudly. "I think it's from reading all your mystery books, Mimi!" Papa howled. "Bucking for an early Christmas gift, little buckaroo?" Grant looked puzzled.

"That's western talk for: are you trying to butter Mimi up?" Christina translated.

"No, I'm not," Grant insisted. He grabbed a piece of bread. "I'm just trying to butter this toast."

As Papa loaded the car, Christina begged Mimi, "Can Grant and I just walk around the corner and see the Alamo one last time? *Please.*"

Mimi looked at her watch. "I don't want to miss our flight," she said. "So hurry. Be back in ten minutes."

Grant and Christina grinned and synchronized their official Carole Marsh Mysteries fan club watches. "That'll be when the big hand gets on the four ghosts," Grant said.

"No ghosts!" Mimi made Grant promise.

As they made their way around the corner, Christina looked up at the beautiful Alamo shrine. Maybe no one will ever know completely what happened here, she thought. After all, everyone who fought and died here was, well, dead.

To The Alamo!

One Last Visit

A surprise note!

"Hey, Grant," she said suddenly. "Get over there in front of the Alamo, and I'll make your picture."

Happily, Grant ran to the front of the building, very carefully avoiding a patch of cactus.

As he posed in one of his usual silly poses, Christina focused the camera. The sun was shining directly on the building, and the sky was bright blue and the patch of grass in front of it was lime green. "This is going to be a great shot," she said aloud to herself.

But just as she started to push the shutter release, something in the upstairs window caught her eye. She took the camera down and looked. Maybe it was just a reflection, she thought, but she swore she saw the little blond-haired boy looking down at her. Could it be the boy the girl said the soldier had saved? Or . . . hmm, perhaps he had not been able to save him, and that's why he still haunted this place. But when she looked back up, the boy was gone—if indeed he had ever been there at all.

"FUZZY PICKLES!" Grant screamed to give himself a big smile.

"Snap! Got it!" said Christina, and they both looked down at their watches. It was time to go. "Not even time to search for gold," Christina lamented. "Oh, well, maybe next time." Then she and Grant hopped

Watch Out...

Missed!

over the Alamo wall and ran back to the hotel to catch
the plane home.

¡Adios!

 Watch Out...  Missed!

About the Author

Carole Marsh is an author and publisher who has written many works of fiction and non-fiction for young readers. She travels throughout the United States and around the world to research her books. In 1979 Carole Marsh was named Communicator of the Year for her corporate communications work with major national and international corporations.

Marsh is the founder and CEO of Gallopade International, established in 1979. Today, Gallopade International is widely recognized as a leading source of educational materials for every state and many countries. Marsh and Gallopade were recipients of the 2004 Teachers' Choice Award. Marsh has written more than 50 Carole Marsh Mysteries™. In 2007, she was named Georgia Author of the Year. Years ago, her children, Michele and Michael, were the original characters in her mystery books. Today, they continue the Carole Marsh Books tradition by working at Gallopade. By adding grandchildren Grant and Christina as new mystery characters, she has continued the tradition for a third generation.

Ms. Marsh welcomes correspondence from her readers. You can e-mail her at fanclub@gallopade.com, visit carolemarshmysteries.com, or write to her in care of Gallopade International, P.O. Box 2779, Peachtree City, Georgia, 30269 USA.

Built-In Book Club
Talk About It!

1. Who was your favorite character? Why?

2. What was your favorite part of the book? Why?

3. What was the scariest part of the book? Why?

4. How do you think the 200 soldiers in the Alamo felt when they faced 6000 Mexican soldiers? Were the Alamo defenders brave or unwise for choosing to fight to the death?

5. Do you like to learn about historical places like the Alamo? Why or why not?

6. Is Christina brave for going into the Alamo chapel alone in the dark? Discuss the difference between bravery, courage, and foolishness.

7. Why is Christina sad about the buildings and businesses that have developed around the Alamo? Discuss the reasons for preserving an historic place.

8. What do you like about reading mysteries?

Built-In Book Club
Bring It to Life!

1. Have a Mexican food fiesta! Ask book club members and their parents to prepare a Mexican dish to share. Can't you just taste the enchiladas, fajitas, tacos, salsa, guacamole, and chimichangas? The possibilities are endless—and delicious!

2. Research the floor plan of the Alamo mission. Draw the floor plan on a poster board. Label each room with a different color. How many rooms were there? Do you think it was pretty crowded with 200 soldiers living there?

3. Are you clueless—or not? After everyone has finished reading the book, divide the book club into two teams. Direct each team to recall as many clues as they can from the book. List each clue, and then write down how each clue makes sense now that everyone knows the end of the story! The team with the most clues is the winner!

4. Create a crossword puzzle! Ask for a volunteer who is willing to create a crossword puzzle using the Spanish glossary words in the book. Pass out the crossword to book club members, and see who finishes (with all the words correct) first!

JUAN & ROSE'S

adiós: *(ah dee oos)* goodbye

aeropuerto: *(air oh pwer toe)* airport

baños: *(bah nyoce)* restrooms

bien: *(bee in)* good; fine; ok

bote: *(bow teh)* boat

buenos días: *(bway nus dee us)* good morning

familia: *(fah me lee ah)* family

hacienda: *(ha see en dah)* main large estate house

hermana: *(er mah nah)* sister

hermano: *(er mah no)* brother

¡hola!: *(oh-luh)* hello

hotel: *(oh tell)* hotel

huevos: *(oo eh vos)* eggs

Spanish Glossary

información: *(in for may see on)* information

leche: *(leh cheh)* milk

libro: *(lee broh)* book

limonada: *(lee moe nah dah)* lemonade

mariachi: *(mah ree ah chee)* Mexican street band

no: *(noh)* no

pan: *(pahn)* bread

por favor: *(poor fah vohr)* please

rojo, blanco, azul: *(row how, blahn koe, ah zool)* red, white, blue

sí: *(see)* yes

sopa: *(sew pah)* soup

teléfono: *(teh leh fo no)* telephone

uno, dos, tres: *(oo no, dose, trehs)* one, two, three

GLOSSARY

amphibious: operating on land and water

columns: tall pillars used in architecture

contraband: illegal, prohibited, or smuggled goods

curator: a person in charge of a library or museum

dingy: dirty and shabby conditions

duel: a formal battle between two people to solve an argument by drawing guns or swords on each other

eccentric: someone who does things strangely or oddly

exasperate: to frustrate or annoy

famished: being really, really, really hungry!

freighters: big ocean-going ships that carry lots of cargo

harbor: bay or gulf where many ships come in and out

hectare: a metric measurement like an acre

hull: the tough outer shell of a ship

illegal: against the law

interrogation: intense questioning on a particular subject

marathon: a long race; a challenge

nonchalantly: doing something with a lack of interest

skeptical: having or showing doubt

synchronize: to cause to move or happen at the same time or speed

triskaidekaphobia: fear of Friday the 13th

vandalize: to destroy or damage property out of a desire to do harm or mischief

Scavenger Hunt

Recipe for fun: Read the book, take the tour, find the items on this list and check them off! (Hint: Look high and low!!) *Teachers: you have permission to reproduce this form for your students.*

___ 1. River Walk

___ 2. Alamo

___ 3. Cenotaph

___ 4. Bridge

___ 5. Hemisphere

___ 6. Alamodome

___ 7. a Spanish word

___ 8. a skeleton key

___ 9. a cactus

___10. any Mexican food item

WOULD YOU ~~CAROLE MARSH MYSTERIES~~ LIKE TO BE
A CHARACTER IN A CAROLE MARSH MYSTERY?

If you would like to star in a Carole Marsh Mystery, fill out the form below and write a 25-word paragraph about why you think you would make a good character! Once you're done, ask your mom or dad to send this page to:

> Carole Marsh Mysteries Fan Club
> Gallopade International
> P.O. Box 2779
> Peachtree City, GA 30269

My name is: _____

I am a: _____boy _____girl   Age: _____

I live at: _____

City: _____ State:____ Zip code: _____

My e-mail address: _____

My phone number is: _____

_____

_____

_____

_____

_____

_____

_____

_____

_____

WRITE YOUR OWN MYSTERY!

Make up a dramatic title!

You can pick four real kid characters!

Select a real place for the story's setting!

Try writing your first draft!

Edit your first draft!

Read your final draft aloud!

You can add art, photos or illustrations!

Share your book with others and send me a copy!

Six Secret Writing Tips from Carole Marsh!

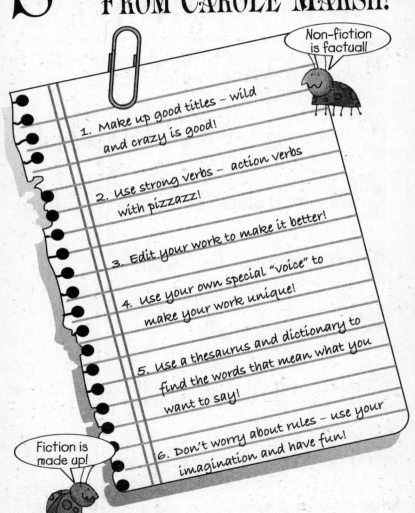

1. Make up good titles – wild and crazy is good!

2. Use strong verbs – action verbs with pizzazz!

3. Edit your work to make it better!

4. Use your own special "voice" to make your work unique!

5. Use a thesaurus and dictionary to find the words that mean what you want to say!

6. Don't worry about rules – use your imagination and have fun!

Non-fiction is factual!

Fiction is made up!

Enjoy this exciting excerpt from

THE MYSTERY AT KILL DEVIL HILLS

1 MAN WILL NEVER FLY

Grant, Christina, Mimi and Papa stood and looked at the little red airplane. It had *My Girl* written on the side in cursive.

"Are we all packed?" Papa asked.

"Everything's stowed away, captain," said Mimi.

Grant and Christina giggled. Their grandfather had only recently gotten his pilot's license and was flying them to North Carolina for the big 100th anniversary of the first flight celebration. It was supposed to be a BIG DEAL, Christina had been told. Her grandmother had been writing books about the Wright brothers' miraculous first manned flight for more than a year.

"Then all aboard!" Papa said.

"Don't you have your planes and your trains all mixed up?" Christina teased Papa.

Papa roared with laughter. "Planes, trains, automobiles, camels, donkeys, rickshaws—whatever it takes, we're going to be in Kill Devil Hills in time for the whole shebang," he promised.

The "whole shebang" was supposed to be everything you could imagine to celebrate the first flight. The President of the United States was coming. So was the aircraft carrier the *Kitty Hawk*. There was going to be a big flyover of all kinds of aircraft. And, most especially, a replica of *Flyer*, Orville and Wilbur Wright's first powered airplane was going to be flown over the enormous sand dunes at Kill Devil Hills.

Of course, thought Christina, Mimi was most excited about the Black and White "First Flight" Ball! Her ball gown was beautiful. Christina sure wished she was going. She looked over at Grant who was all strapped in and wide-eyed. He had never flown in a plane this small and he looked a little scared.

"It's ok, Grant," Christina told her younger brother, who was seven. Christina was nine and liked to think she had seen it all, although she knew she had not. However, she had seen a lot since she and her brother often gallivanted around America with their grandparents. Mimi wrote mystery books for kids and often included her grandchildren, their friends, and members of her Carole Marsh Mysteries fan club in the books.

They had been to a lot of neat places, almost always having fun, and almost always getting in trouble before it was over with. Of course, Mimi usually put all that in the books, so it was ok. She called it "research." Grant and Christina called it getting out of school with a neat excuse!

On this trip to the Outer Banks of North Carolina, they were going to meet up with their Tarheel cousins Griffin and Alex.

Griffin was 10 and Alex was 12. They were a lot of fun to be around. Christina envied them because they got to live at the beach year-round. They always had tans and windblown hair. They knew how to surf and hang glide and all that beachy keen stuff. Christina hoped they would teach her some of that this year. She was not used to going to the beach in the winter, though. Why couldn't Orville and Wilbur have made their famous first flight in the summer, she thought.

Suddenly, Papa started the engines up and the little propellers began to spin. The Halloween orange windsock at Falcon Field seem to satisfy Papa that "all systems were go," as he said. Christina thought her grandfather would have made a good astronaut.

As the little plane began to crawl, then run, then speed across the tarmac, Grant grabbed his sister by the hand.

"Hey," he yelled over the noise. "Don't Mimi and Papa belong to the Man Will Never Fly Something or the Other?"

"Yes, they do," Christina screamed back at him. "It's a club." The adults in front could not even hear them.

"Then," said Grant, "if man will never fly, what are we doing in this contraption?"

Christina laughed. "Oh, Grant, you've flown on airplanes before. Lots of times."

"I kknow," said Grant, his voice stuttering as the plane's wheels seemed to bounce across the runway. "Bbut they were BIG. This thing ffeels llike a rocking horse."

Christina held her brother's hand tighter as the airplane suddenly swooshed smoothly up into the air. A little turbulence rocked them left and right as they pulled up into the sky. As Papa banked the plane and began a turn over the beautiful forested city where they lived—Peachtree City, Georgia—Grant seemed to relax. He let his sister's hand drop and reared back and stretched and yawned as though the takeoff had been a piece of cake.

"I guess man will fly," Grant admitted.

"Well, thousands of people are sure counting on it in North Carolina this week," Christina said, fishing around in her backpack for some peanuts. You can't fly without eating peanuts, can you, she wondered to herself.

As he leveled the airplane out, Papa glanced back at his two grandchildren. "Orville and Wilbur, here we come!" he said.

Everyone, including Mimi, laughed. That's because they had no way of knowing that they were flying into the strangest mystery they had ever encountered and that the fate of the BIG DEAL celebration would be all up to four kids. And even now, the clock was ticking.

Enjoy this exciting excerpt from

THE MYSTERY OF BILTMORE HOUSE

1 FOUR HOT, SWEATY, CRAZY, MAD KIDS

Stacy Brown dealt the cards into the sloppy stacks in the back seat of the red station wagon. She snapped each card with as loud a pop as she could. She was mad.

"That sure doesn't sound like homework," her mom commented from the front seat.

Snap. "School's". . . pop . . ."out," Stacy reminded her.

Her mom mumbled and Stacy mumbled back. School was out, and all of her friends were starting their part-time summer jobs. All except her. And here she was stuck in Asheville on her way to Biltmore House where she had been a hundred . . . thousand . . . million times before. Just because her mom had to help coordinate a mystery writing workshop being held at the estate this week.

Stacy had a part-time job at a kennel all lined up. She needed money badly. There was an international dog show in California, where she used to live, the next week. And, boy, did she want to go. Shoot, she'd been showing dogs since she was a puppy herself. She'd won lots of prizes. But this worldwide meet would be just wonderful. The time was right. It was for kids just her age, thirteen. And her dog was in perfect condition.

Her mom always said you have to make things happen. So Stacy had worked hard to get that job to make enough money to go. But now her mom was making her tag along with her like she was a baby or something.

Next to showing dogs, Stacy's favorite thing was playing bridge. But it didn't seem like much fun today in the hot, sweaty back seat playing all four hands by herself.

Stacy saw her mom look at her in the rearview mirror. *Spy*, Stacy thought. I'm being watched. She could see her mom frown at her windblown hair and her skirt that was wrinkled from sprawling in a not-too-ladylike position, trying to make room for invisible bridge partners. Stacy turned her face where her mom couldn't see it and made an awful face.

Why did they have to meet the others here at historic Biltmore Village? Why couldn't they have met them at the McDonald's across the street where they had civilization—milk shakes?

The blue Mustang sped down I-26 toward the mountains. He's gonna get a ticket, the boy in the back seat thought. He stared up into the sky looking for a blue light to come from outer space and pull them over. Nothing. Shucks.

Trent Evans swiped a thin streak of perspiration above his lip. "Air," he moaned dramatically from the back seat. "Air!"

He pretended he was being kidnapped and held hostage. Didn't that happen recently somewhere between Spartanburg and Asheville? Any minute he was going to be tossed in the trunk where summer had been stored since last year. Maybe his dad could put that in a mystery story.

Somehow, while all his friends were heading the opposite direction, toward the cool South Carolina coast, he was trapped into going with his dad to a writing workshop in Asheville.

He didn't even know his dad wanted to be a writer. He wasn't a writer. He was an engineer. But the textile plant he worked for had some temporary layoffs. His dad was always telling him when life gives you lemons, make lemonade. And so he had decided that instead of moping around the house worrying about lost hours, he would try his hand at writing.

Trent was sure it had all been his mother's idea. He knew that it had been her idea that this would be a great time for father and son to get to know each other better.

Trent sank back into the hot cushion and watched the mountains get larger before his very eyes. "I'll bet I could get to know Dad real good at the beach," he muttered. "Besides, if you don't know your dad by the time you're eleven, when are you supposed to know him?"

Wendy and Michael Hunt sat glumly in the back seat of the car. They were both hunched over some of Mother's long pads of yellow paper. Michael was inventing a new video game where a horrid monster gobbled up big sisters. Wendy was writing notes about which cute fourth grade girl Michael was in love with to pay him back.

Suddenly, the car swerved left, then right, tossing their papers out of their hands. Mother never takes the straight route, Wendy thought. We could have gotten on the interstate and made it from Tryon to Asheville in thirty minutes. But if there was a long way around, Mother always took it.

Mother's camera equipment and trusty rusty typewriter were piled up on the seat beside her. She never went anywhere without either one. "A tornado might come charging down the road and I wouldn't want to miss it," she would always say. I can just picture her making a picture of us getting scooped up by some big black inverted triangle, Wendy thought.

Michael was mad, too. It had been his turn to ride in the front. But they had argued about it and so Mother had pointed them both to the back seat. It was going to be a long, hot summer, he decided. And what a way to start—going to a big, old house so his mother could attend a writing workshop. She'd written a bunch of books—why did she need more courses, he wondered. Then he remembered. She wasn't taking a class, she was teaching one. As if being a mother weren't bad enough, now she was going to be a teacher, too. The thought of the combination gave him cold chills up his hot backbone.

At precisely the same time, two cars whipped into the steaming asphalt parking places beside Stacy's car. A white car on the left; a blue one on the right. She felt like she was in the middle of a twelve-wheeled American flag. A fast glimpse showed her there was one boy in one car and a boy and girl in the other. A foursome for bridge, she thought. Then she frowned. They probably didn't like cards. They probably won't like me. And I'll bet they don't want to be here any more than I do.

The adults all hopped out of the cars and met on the sidewalk. Stacy could tell from the nodding and shaking of hands that introductions were being made all around. The kids just sat in the cars and stared meanly at ßone another, as though it was the others' fault they were here.

The adults chuckled. As her mom got back in the car, Stacy heard her say loudly enough for the kids to hear, "I have the perfect thing to cheer this hot bunch up before we head for Biltmore House."

Stacy scooped all her cards into a pile and stacked them up in record time. As if she was jumping hurdles, she bounded over the seats into the front one beside her mom. She knew what that meant.

Trent stared at the crazy girl in the car next to him. He was puzzled by her hopping around. Then he was even more puzzled when she waved gaily at him.

Wendy and Michael looked through the steamy window at the strange girl in the next car. She turned and smiled at them. "Whatever she's got to be happy about is a mystery to me," Wendy muttered.

Spreading the tips of his fingers up to the edge of the window, Michael waved and smiled back at the mysterious-acting girl.

VISIT THE CAROLE MARSH MYSTERIES WEBSITE

www.carolemarshmysteries.com

- *Check out what's coming up next! Are we coming to your area with our next book release? Maybe you can have your book signed by the author!*

- *Join the Carole Marsh Mysteries Fan Club!*

- *Apply for the chance to be a character in an upcoming Carole Marsh Mystery!*

- *Learn how to write your own mystery!*